BIN LADEN'S BALD SPOT

BIN LADEN'S BALD SPOT
& OTHER STORIES

BRIAN DOYLE

 RED HEN PRESS | *Pasadena, CA*

Book layout by Andrew Mendez

ISBN: 978-1-59709-179-4 (eBook)
ISBN: 978-1-59709-461-0 (hardcover)
ISBN: 978-1-59709-915-8 (tradepaper)

Library of Congress Cataloging-in-Publication Data

Doyle, Brian, 1956 Nov. 6-
  Bin Laden's bald spot & other stories / Brian Doyle. —1st ed.
    p. cm.
  ISBN 978-1-59709-915-8 (tradepaper)
  I. Title.
  PS3604.O9547B56 2011
  813'.6—dc22
                        2011013319

The Los Angeles County Arts Commission, the National Endowment for the
Arts, the California Arts Council and Los Angeles Department of Cultural
Affairs partially support Red Hen Press.

First Edition
Published by Red Hen Press
www.redhen.org

ACKNOWLEDGEMENTS

Most of these peculiar tales first appeared in magazines and such, and I thank the editors of same for printing my fictive misadventures. Brave editors, them editors.

"AAA Plus" appeared in *Harper's* magazine, all due respect and bowing gratefully to the deft editor Elizabeth Giddens.

"Ramon Martinez . . . " appeared in *The Sun*, that subtle & startling magazine published in North Carolina by Sy Safransky. Most sincere thanks to his skinny relentless cheerful Synergy. "Ramon" then appeared in *Opium* magazine, thanks to Ian Bassingthwaighte, a Wodehousean moniker if ever I heard one.

"The Boyfriends Bus" appeared in *Harvard Review*, courtesy of editor Christina Thompson.

"The Cuckold 10K" and "The Train" were in *Natural Bridge* (Volumes 7 and 10, respectively), which is published at the University of Missouri-Saint Louis. Special thanks to then-editor David Carkeet, who is a heck of a fine novelist, you know. If you have never read his baseball novel *The Greatest Slump of All Time* do so. It's hilarious and poignant.

"Hurtgen" appeared in *U.S. Catholic*, where it won a 2007 Catholic Press Association Award, which was pretty cool, although there was no beer in it for me, and I thank editor Meinrad Scherer-Emunds for letting it through the inky door. "Lucy," "Blue," "Waking the Bishop," and "Yoda" also appeared in *U.S. Catholic*, and my particular thanks to editors Maureen Abood, Cathy O'Connell-Cahill, and Heidi Schlumpf.

"Stay Flush" appeared in *Mary* magazine from Saint Mary's College in Moraga, California, which is a lovely place altogether, the crisp and brilliant air, the mountains in the distance, the grinning students.

The funky webzine *Smokebox*, edited by the bizarre writers Marc Covert and John Richen, printed, or posted, "Malo" and "A Confession." Listen, when you are done reading this book, go hit the web for *Smokebox* and read through their hilarious and angry and eloquent archive of David James Duncan stuff. One of the great writers in the U S of A, Duncan is, despite his taste for the foul mud-puddle swill called Scottish whiskey.

"Mule," which first appeared in *Flyway*, the literary journal from Iowa State University (thanks to discerning young editor Alaura Wilfert), then also appeared in *Smokebox*, with a haunting piece of art by John Richen.

"The Fox" appeared in *The Pinch*, a journal published by writing students at the University of Memphis; the journal's title is from an old neighborhood of that seething city, so called because of the starving Irish immigrants who once flooded it. Prayers on those frightened brave exiled souls, ravenous and weary.

"King of the Losers" appeared in *New Letters*, edited by the excellent essayist Robert Stewart; *New Letters* is published at the University of Missouri at Kansas City. For fun visit www.newletters.org.

"Chino's Story" appeared in *River & Sound Review*, thanks to Jay Bates and Julie Case, and "Do You Think We Should Pull Over?" appeared in *The Kenyon Review*, thanks to David Lynn and Andre Bernard.

for my brother
John Kevin Doyle

TABLE OF CONTENTS

BIN LADEN'S BALD SPOT

BIN LADEN'S BALD SPOT

Only two men in this sweet bruised world know that Osama bin Laden, son of Alia Ghanem and Muhammad bin Laden, has under his turban a sprightly crewcut modeled on Van Johnson in the 1954 movie *The Last Time I Saw Paris*, which, as only a few other men know, is his favorite movie, or used to be before he had to give up electronics for various excellent reasons. I have also heard him say, more than once, as I cut his hair, that *The Caine Mutiny* with Van Johnson is his favorite movie, so I think we may conclude safely that his favorite movie is one in which Van Johnson is a featured player, although it may be that Osama, all due respect to the Vanster, has a thing for crewcuts rather than cinema.

Also I am here to tell you that Osama has a bald spot the size of a baby's fist on the back of his head, shaped *exactly* like Iceland, complete with the Vestfjarda Peninsula to the west. He does *not* like to speak of this and indeed we have only spoken of it once, when I said to him, sir, you have a bald spot back here shaped like Iceland, and he said I do *not*, and I said, yes sir, you do, it is the size of my fist and even has the little peninsula to the west, you know, like Iceland does, and he said I do *not* have a bald spot, and I said, yes sir, well sir, actually yes you do, sir, it's a big honking thing, too, and I remember learning the names of the towns in Iceland for extra credit when I was in school, many years ago, Borgarfjardharsysla and Eyjafjardharsysla and Hafnarfjordhur and Isafjordhur and of course Snaefellsnessysla-og-Hnappadalssysla, is that a cool name or what, who could forget such a name, and the fact is that your bald spot is really amazingly like Iceland complete with the Vestfjarda Peninsula to the west, so maybe we should be discussing a hair weave? Sir?

Well, after that I was forbidden to speak at all in any manner whatsoever in his presence, although I am still allowed in to the cave complex every Wednesday for haircuts, first Osama and then in descending hierarchical order all other men, who also get crew-cuts, it's like being the barber for a high school football team with major weaponry.

The other men speak to me animatedly when Himself is out of earshot getting made up for his endless film productions, and it is a great surprise to me how many of them think that Van Johnson was never more than a decent supporting player, no matter what Osama thinks, and, as they say quietly, the fact is that liking the way a guy wears *his* hair because you are paranoid about *your* hair does *not* make the guy the greatest actor who ever lived, no matter *how* vehemently you hold the opinion or think yourself a visionary in cultural or religious or geopolitical matters, because the greatest actor who ever lived is inarguably Cary Grant, although one of the men holds out adamantly for Gregory Peck, which sends the rest of them into hysterics.

One time I was doing a hurried series of crewcuts for the men, there was some film production emergency they had to attend to, something about Osama's new combat jacket not being properly pre-rumpled for the video, and they got into the whole Gregory Peck argument, which led to a sight I will never forget as long as I live, which was seven men with crewcuts in a cave imitating that stiff wooden walk of Gregory Peck's, you know, like in *Roman Holiday* with Audrey Hepburn, when he looks like he is auditioning to play Frankenstein or something, so anyway we were all giggling when Osama himself appeared suddenly, and for a moment we thought it was curtains for sure, whereas the Leader, all due respect, doesn't have a single humor neuron in his body, but it turned out *he thought we were trying to emulate him*, and it tells you something about Osama that he thought that seven men walking like robots and sniggering like bandits were doing their level best to be as cool as he thinks he is.

Since that time I have endeavored to persuade the men that having me shave bald spots in the shape of Iceland onto their crania, complete with the Vestfjarda Peninsula to the west, would be *really* funny, but they have so far declined, although I have pointed out that their turbans would of course cover the spots, and it would be a collective private joke in the same vein as the occasional Gregory Peck walk they do when Osama is outside scouting suitable sets for his endless videos, but they have so far declined, although I am a man filled with hope, like old Gregory Peck in *To Kill a Mockingbird*, when he insists that there is justice in this world against all evidence, which I believe is true, because even though I am only a barber, I know that the men who sit quietly under my clippers will someday pay for the crimes they have committed, and their leader, if they can pry him away from the video camera, will pay for the pain he has caused; and when that time comes, whether in this world or the next, I will pack my barbering tools in their supple leather case, and emerge from these caves blinking in the light, and go rent every Van Johnson movie ever made, and laugh out loud every time old Van reaches up to confirm the arrogant blade of his hair, or mugs for the camera, or tries desperately to be the hero, although he knows and we know that he is only a flickering ephemera, a creature of the dark, a thing that squirms and quails and dies when pierced by the brilliant snarl of the sun.

KING OF THE LOSERS

My sister and her boyfriend have two kids, girls, ages four and one. The kids are total sweethearts and the big one is wicked smart and can read already. My sister is wicked smart too but she has major mental thunderstorms and the social service has come three times to check on the kids. The boyfriend is messed up too but his problem is simply that he is the biggest loser ever. The best job he ever had was delivering pizza which lasted two whole days before they fired him and docked all his pay, which tells you all you need to know. His job these days as far as I can tell is stealing money from countertops and mailboxes. My other sister and I used to leave dollar bills on the kitchen counter and bet how fast he would palm them. His all-time record was nineteen seconds. If there really was a God this guy would be working in a prison laundry but there's clearly no God or not much of one because my sister is always talking how much she loves the guy but we see him for what he is, which is king of the losers. I would beat him up but what's the point? My sister would just fawn over the bruises and he would be so mortified that a teenager hammered him that he would be even meaner to his kids, and I love those kids.

Anyway the point of my story is the fourth time the social services came to their house, which is a total pit. My sister isn't capable of maintaining the house and the loser is too lazy. They don't pay rent or anything on the house. The loser got it from his uncle as a tax dodge. For a long time my mom and dad and other sister and I would go over on the weekends and clean up just to keep the kids from living in filth but my dad quit going over because he always ends up crying or my sister screaming at him and my mom is all busy with the courts trying to get custody of the kids, and my other sister moved away and got a crewcut and changed her name, so I am the only one going over there lately.

So the other day I drive over to clean the bathroom and kitchen, which are the absolute crucial places to clean, but when I get there the social service truck is parked in front of the house and I get the willies, because three times is the limit for social service and the fourth time is business.

I can hear the loser yelling and my sister hysterical, so I go around back and find the girls on the swings, the big one pushing the little one. I ask them how long the social service has been here and the older one says like only two minutes because she and her sister just came out and she remembered to buckle the baby into the swing like I showed her. I say that is excellent baby management and they can swing for exactly one minute while I check the score, and I lean in the back door and hear the calm reasonable voices of the social service and the loser yelling that they are his kids dammit and this is fascism and where's the warrant and he knows his rights and this is a police state and etc. I listen for my sister but now I don't hear her at all, which is a bad sign; when she's really flipped out she shuts down all systems and erects deflector shields and rocks herself in the closet.

So I realize this is doomsday, social service has come to take the kids, and while I totally support the idea of social service, and how the state is responsible for children from untenable homes, I also know these are sort of my kids too, so I gather up the girls and we cut across the neighbors' yards and slip into my car like secret agent spies, me carrying the baby like a football which she thinks is funny, and we drive away very quietly and go five towns before we stop and get some fries and try to think this puppy through.

My dad is a math teacher and he taught us that major problems are best solved by breaking them into components, so I calculate details first, money and gas and food and diapers and the chances of the social service coming after me or calling my parents or maybe even putting the loser in jail, and I conclude we're screwed, especially as re diapers.

Right about then there's a ketchup incident and the baby starts to cry and the manager is staring at us so we retreat to the car, but as soon as we are on the road the four year old tells me the baby needs to be changed, she can tell, and we stop and get diapers and then stop at a park where I change the baby on the grass because the bathroom is locked with a huge padlock that I can't get off even after using a tire iron to try to break it off. I mean, why lock a public bathroom, you know? The point of a public bathroom is that it's public, right? Talk about your social services.

Finally we get back on the road and head toward the beach figuring in winter there won't be anybody there and we can haul up and take stock of the situation.

We go to the beach? says the four year old. Her name is Ari.

You know this road? I say.

One time our car broke here, she says.

What a shock, I think, the losermobile breaking down.

It was fun, she said. We saw fish. Daddy had beer.

Did he?

Beer is important.

Is that so?

Daddy says so.

Okay.

Baby sleeping.

Good, I say. Are you tired, Ari?

I never tired. Sleeping for babies.

Okay.

We go swimming?

Too cold. We'll go swimming in summer.

Is summer tomorrow?

A few weeks.

Can I have more fries?

You can eat the rest of the bag.

Thank you, Kenny.

You're welcome, Ari.

When we get to the beach we park behind the old bathhouse they are still fixing two years after they started because there was a huge scandal with the money. It was in the papers. This reminds me of some of the loser's greatest hits, like one time my other sister caught him with our dad's wallet in his hand and the loser says he was checking dad's birth date, or the time the guy across the street got tired of the loser going through his mailbox for checks and he put a monster rat trap in his mailbox and it nearly tore the loser's fingers off and the loser told us he hurt his hand fighting off a mugger, or the time my other sister caught him taking the money she left for Ari to get snacks at preschool. That time she slapped him good, and he cocked his fist and I stood up fast and he backed off. That was the only time she ever lost it with the loser. She left home four days later.

I check Ari and I see she's asleep too and I gauge the immediate future. I have a bank card and can hit the machine for three hundred, the daily maximum. Food we can get, diapers we have, and there's plenty of gas. I try to think about the component of the problem where a guy sixteen years old is totally on the lam with a child age four and a child age one, but Does Not Compute comes up on the mental screen so I listen to the radio for a while until the baby wakes up crying.

The baby waking up wakes up Ari and Ari says the baby is hungry, she can tell.

What do we feed her?

Animal crackers when she crying.

Do we have any?

In my pink coat.

Where's your pink coat?

At home.

I suggest to Ari that maybe more fries will hold the baby over until we get some crackers, and that going back to the house is not a great idea, but she says the baby hates fries and that she, Ari, loves her coat, and also the baby's binky is on the grass by the swings and without binky she will never stop crying, so I put the car in gear and ease out from behind the old bathhouse, but just then the losermobile fishtails right in front of us and the loser jumps out yelling and runs right at us before I can hit the brakes, and we hit him medium hard and he goes head over heels right over the car like my dad says a deer did when he was driving my mom to the hospital to have my first sister. The way my dad tells it is that the deer crushed the top of the car so he and my mom had to drive to the hospital crouched down in the front seat peering at the road, but that this was actually a good thing because a few inches the other way and that would have been the end of my mom and dad and sister.

Daddy flying, says Ari.

Dumbo, says the baby clear as day.

I grab the tire iron as I get out of the car, just in case, but it turns out there's no need, the loser is totally out cold with his face in a puddle, so I break the problem down into components. What I need primarily at the moment is animal crackers and binky, so I drag the loser out of the puddle and fold him into the trunk and lock it and head down the road looking for a store.

We find one but they don't have animal crackers and the baby won't eat the ginger snaps I get on sale for $1.99, a huge bag, how they can make money selling such a big bag for so little money is a mystery to me, but then we do find a grocery store with a whole wall of animal crackers, it's like the motherlode of animal crackers, so I buy twenty boxes just to be safe. These are $2.09 each. Ari and I open two boxes and count the crackers. There are twenty in each box, so I point out to Ari that the crackers are like ten cents each, see? Whereas the ginger snaps are about a penny each, the bag being the size of a puppy chow bag.

She just don't like the gingers, Kenny.

Okay, honey.

By this time the loser is awake and yelling and banging in the trunk so we get back on the road.

Daddy mad, says Ari.

He's not a happy man, I say.

He yelling.

I hear him.

You give Daddy a time out.

I did, Ari.

Where is Mommy?

She's home.

We go home?

Where exactly is your pink coat, Ari?

Behind the back door. I hang it on the nail. Mommy says it belongs on the nail, not on the floor.

We'll go get your coat.

I love my coat.

And we'll get the binky.

She love binky.

When we get near the house I tell Ari to duck down like a secret agent spy and guard the spaceship while I get the magic coat and she says Aye Captain and I slip back to the house through the back yards and find the coat right on the nail where she says it is. That Ari is the coolest kid ever. She learned to read by figuring out the letters on the backs of the books at our house, and then she started reading comic strips in the papers, and pretty soon she was reading captions on news photographs. She was the one who told me about the scandal with the money with the bathhouse, because the word bathhouse fascinated her and she wanted to know why there were certain houses that were only for taking baths.

I listen for my sister but I don't hear anything so I scribble a note that the kids are okay and the loser is not in jail yet and hang it on the nail and slip back to the car. Ari says the loser has been yelling and banging so loud that the baby started to cry and so she, Ari, gave the baby more animal crackers.

That is excellent, Ari, I say. Good baby management.

Daddy hungry too, she says.

Did he tell you that?

Yes he did, Kenny.

Can you hear him through the seat?

Through the hole.

What hole?

The elbow pillow hole, she says, and she shows me that when you fold down the centerpiece of the back seat there is indeed a circular hole the size of a baseball between the trunk and the back seat, I guess for ventilation. As soon as Ari shows me the hole, though, the loser starts yelling through it so we close it up again.

Can I give Daddy an animal cracker? asks Ari.

Better save those for the baby.

Ginger snap?

Okay. Just one, though.

She waits a minute for him to stop yelling and then she opens the pillow real fast and pops a ginger snap into it and then slams it shut again before he can start yelling, and we get back on the road.

I figure the best thing overall is to keep moving. My dad says the coolest thing about mathematics is not that there are fixed and immutable answers to problems, this is a popular misconception about the subtle genius and deep attraction of mathematics, but it's the other way around, nothing is fixed and secure, all things are in motion at all times, so mathematics is actually a living language for describing where things are at any particular moment, but that any statement of absolute truth is intrinsically and by nature inaccurate, which is why politics, for example, is theater and not science. My mom gets impatient when he rambles along in this vein because she says there are some immutable truths and the point of life is to grapple with what is rather than go all moony and flabby about subjectivity and relativity. One time when my mom was having a particularly bad day with my first sister, my other sister deliberately asked for an example of an immutable truth just to set mom off, and mom, totally taking the bait, said For example the fact that your sister is addicted to a selfish and abusive wastrel, which then became a catch phrase for me and my other sister as re the loser.

It seems to me that we will be hardest to spot in a sea of cars so we take the expressway and then the belt parkway around the city because there is a circus or something downtown and we don't want to get stuck. As we go over the bridge Ari looks for elephants for the baby but doesn't see any. When we get out in the country we stop for lunch and Ari says we better wear the baby out before her nap otherwise she won't nap more than an hour and will be all cranky. So we spend a couple hours at a park by a river where there's an excellent playground with wood chips under the monkey bars and swings. Wood chips underneath play structures seem like an excellent idea to me, although Ari says you can get splinters from them if you fall the wrong way, her friends Melanie and Melody got splinters from the wood chips at school, but teacher took the splinters out right away and Melanie and Melody both got cool bandaids and cookies. Also Melody was faking a little.

When we get back to the car I see that the loser has kicked dents in the trunk from the inside and the car looks like it has hives. This is not good, because the last thing my mom and dad need at this point is to worry about the car, but to be honest I can understand how the loser would be a little frustrated with his day so far, not to mention he is wet from the puddle, so I go to give him a ginger snap through the hole but he tries to grab my hand and I have to hit his fingers with the tire iron.

I figure this is as good a time as any to have a talk with him and I tell him through the hole that matters are in hand, we have diapers and animal crackers and the kids are not with social service, which is where they would be if he was captain of the ship.

Aye Captain, says Ari.

The girls each say Hello Daddy to the hole and Ari tries to give him another ginger snap but he tries to grab her hand also and I have to crack him again with the tire iron. One thing about the loser is he is not the brightest star in the sky. My dad says there are saloon doors with more intellectual capacity than the petty hoodlum with whom his daughter has chosen to cohabit, which is a good example of the way my dad speaks.

Before we get back on the road we stop at a grocery and I hit the machine for the daily maximum and really stock up this time, animal crackers (on sale for $1.89), milk, sandwiches, diapers, sleeping bags, water, bananas, because who doesn't like bananas? and those little oranges that are so easy to peel, you know, the kind that only arrive in stores in winter? Ari says they are from Spain but I am not sure.

Can we go to Spain? she asks.

Someday.

Can we go tomorrow?

We'll see.

Do that mean no?

No.

We should get beer, says Ari. Beer is important.

This is actually not a bad idea, although technically I cannot buy beer, but the checker is clearly no older than me and one thing I have learned from my mom is that if you carry a persona with absolute conviction you are that person, so we choose beer cans that will fit through the hole and I exude confidence and the checker checks them through without comment, in fact she doesn't even look at me and doesn't say anything except paper or plastic?

When we get back to the car the sun is going down and we take a vote on where to go. Ari and I vote for driving into the sun, just because, and the baby gets all excited and says yub yub so we figure that's unanimous. We each have an animal cracker to celebrate the advent of the voyage, as my dad would say, and we give the loser a beer through the hole. I suggest to Ari that every time we cross a state line we give the loser a beer and she says okay but we should give him two beers when we cross into the biggest states of all. It's a mark of how cool Ari is that she knows Texas and California are the biggest states. You can't tell me there are a lot of four-year-olds who know their states that well. I point out that technically Alaska is a huge state also and she agrees that Alaska should count so off we go.

AAA PLUS

One night my car broke down and died not a mile from the shop where I had just spent more than eight hundred dollars on a new starter and timing mechanism and assorted other holy mysteries, and after I coasted it choking and lurching to the side of the road, and sat there silently banging the steering wheel so hard that my wrist still hurts on rainy days, and stepped out squelching into the mud, and hitched home in the furious summer rain, cars swerving and honking and one guy even giving me the finger, I called AAA to get them to tow the car back to the shop, because I couldn't call my wife anymore, whereas she doesn't live with me and the kids anymore, but the tow truck guy refused to tow the car that far because my coverage was only AAA standard, not AAA Plus, which your AAA Plus allows us to tow cars anywhere in these United States, said the tow truck driver, you could tow a car from Alaska to Florida technically, but your AAA standard coverage limits your emergency towing capability to three miles or less, that's the way it is, he said, and he was about as big as a house, so I declined to argue, and he towed the car three miles down the road and was going to leave it there by the side of the highway in accordance with the AAA standard coverage limit, but I swore to high heaven that I would immediately purchase AAA Plus, even doing so retroactively if he thought that necessary, such was my good opinion of his professional judgment in this matter, and he took the compliment and took pity and took my car to my house, where my children poured out to watch his truck, which was indeed a majorly large truck, as one of my sons said.

So next day I purchase AAA Plus, which takes effect immediately upon issuance of your major credit card, says the operator politely, so we seal the deal and when I hang up the phone I am a member of AAA Plus.

I actually felt different, no joke. I felt taller.

So I call the tow truck guy again and he comes back to tow my car back to the shop where I got the new starter and timing mechanism and such. He's cheerful as a jaybird now that I have AAA Plus. He can tow me from here to kingdom fecking come, he says. He can tow me from sea to fecking sea. His name is Denny too, he says, and he is a towing fool. *You Blow, We Tow* is written in letters a foot high on the side of his truck.

I've towed everything with an engine, he says. They all break down in the end. Cars, trucks, boats, ski-doos, even a biplane one time, this old guy dressed like fecking Charles A. Lindbergh landed his plane in a supermarket parking lot and hit a shopping cart and wrecked his plane and I had to tow him home. Guy was wearing a scarf and goggles and everything. The whole nine yards. Must have been eighty years old if he was a day. I tell you, the things I seen! One time I towed a car with a naked guy. Guy was driving around naked when his car blew. I made him stay in the car when I towed it. Which is illegal, but I didn't want a naked guy in my cab. I'd like to see the cop who'd give me a ticket for *that*. Another time I towed a guy who I found out later he just robbed a diner but his car died after like three blocks, but he called for a tow, is that hilarious or what? Guy had AAA Plus too. Another time I towed a guy who when he opened his trunk looking for a jack or something I see his trunk was full of guns. I didn't say anything to anyone about that. You rat a guy like that he comes and shoots you in the face. I don't need trouble. I got enough trouble. We all got troubles. You got troubles?

I got troubles, I say.

People think when you drive a tow truck you must get the girls, says Denny, because you have to tow women of course, I mean half the world is women, right, and their cars are always breaking down because they don't change the oil, they just don't, I don't know why, and a little smoke coming out of the hood freaks them out totally, but you take a guy, a guy would drive with fecking *flames* shooting out of his car, he would probably think that was cool, you know what I'm saying?

A guy, I say, would *speed up* to make the flames look cooler.

That's exactly correct, says Denny. That's absolutely fecking so.

At that point the guy from the repair shop comes out to tell me that my car will need another thousand bucks worth of repairs now, even though they just got finished fixing it, or *saying* they fixed it, and he says what do you want to do? and I say I don't want to *do* anything, you owe me a car I can drive away from this crime scene after the *last* five hundred bucks I spent here, and he says it's not their fault it's a piece of shit car that hasn't been properly maintained, and I say hey, I am not paying another cent for repairs that don't repair, and he says okay, fine, they'll junk it, and I say okay, fine, junk it then, it's junk now anyway since you guys mangled it, and he stomps off, so there I am, up a creek and carless.

Denny gives me a ride home to the kids, whereas I have AAA Plus now and am golden, and he says in fact he can tow the car from the repair shop to my house if I want, whereas I have AAA Plus, and it's a shame to leave a perfectly good car someplace ratty like that, which is true, so the next day he comes and gets me and we get the car and he tows it back to my house. That was a Saturday and the kids were going bonkers because I was supposed to take them up the mountain skiing and now we couldn't go. But Denny, who turned out to be a good guy, says hell, you got AAA Plus, man, you are golden, I can tow you from here to fecking kingdom come, which includes of course the mountain.

The kids thought this was hilarious and they throw their stuff in the trunk and pile in the car and get in a huge argument about who gets to sit behind the steering wheel and who gets to ride shotgun and who is the total loser in the back seat. I ride in the truck with Denny and he tows the car with the kids in it all the way up the mountain, which is like a hundred miles away, and we ski all day and nobody breaks an arm or anything, and then Denny tows us to a little restaurant he knows on the east side of the mountain, where all the truckers go for the best pies and fries, and then late at night he tows us all home again, the kids all asleep in the car.

That was a really great day and the kids still talk about it. We were going to do that once a month or so with Denny but a little later he got a job driving long haul and he sold his tow truck to a guy who didn't want to do AAA so that was the end of fecking that. But I still have my card, and that was a really great day, and I got this story out of it, so that's good, right?

THE BOYFRIENDS BUS

My wife had, by her count, eleven boyfriends before she married me twenty years ago. The way she tells the story it starts with a hockey player in high school who groped her at the prom, and it ends with the guy she lived with for five years before me, and includes such guys as the guy who she was dating who made a pass at a friend of hers, and a guy she dated for four days in Texas, and a guy who used to take her to the beach and photograph her naked there for artistic purposes, and a guy who dumped her for a girl in his Bible class, and a guy who ran a steam shovel, and a guy she went out with because she liked his mustache, and a guy who turned out to have another girlfriend the whole time she was dating him, and some other guys. She doesn't count guys she had crushes on who didn't have crushes on her, of which there were several, and I don't think she is counting guys with whom she made out once in the movies or in a basement for an hour, but I don't ask about that, because who am I to ask, and there are certain levels of detail you don't actually want to be up on, so to speak, you know what I mean?

Anyway over the years she has told plenty of stories about her boyfriends, many of them funny stories, although some of the stories, especially the ones she tells a lot, are not so much funny as cathartic and ultimately self-explanatory, the sort of stories you tell about other people when you are really trying to tell a story about yourself, you know? Stories about how you came to be who you are, which has a lot to do with the lovers you used to have. If you look at the whole boyfriend and girlfriend thing with a long view you see that the system is a total mess; basically you screw up time after time until you get married, if you get married, and then you screw up on a major-league basis, and can't quit as easily.

Sometimes you go out with people you know aren't right for you because you want to see what's it like to go out with people you know you shouldn't go out with, and sometimes you go out with people because they like you and you like that even though you don't like them, or because they have cool cars, or because there's sex in the air, or because they're not at *all* like the boyfriend you just had, and someone not like the last boyfriend looks pretty good when you are reeling from dumping or being dumped by the last boyfriend, and sometimes you go out with someone because they asked you to and you can't think of any good reason to say no, and sometimes you go out with someone because that's the only person who said yes when *you* asked, and sometimes you go out with some-one for the *feeling* of going out with that person, which if you think about it is really a way to see how *you* feel rather than any serious attempt to see how *they* feel, which is why that particular kind of relationship is doomed.

Anyway over the years my wife has told me enough stories about the boyfriends that after a while I began to think of them as real people, which of course they were, and one day by purest chance I ran into one of her old boyfriends, I'll call him Nine, who turned out to be a good guy, a little regretful that he had a chance to marry my wife but didn't really grab for the brass ring, but that was many years and many miles ago as he said, as he bought me a pint, and we got to talking about her other old boyfriends, whom he too had heard stories about, and after we had two pints each he proposed that we convene an old boyfriends meeting, gathering each of the twelve boyfriends, including me, for what would certainly be a pe-culiar and humorous event, and really it would be a celebration of my wife, when you think about it, he said, because we had all in our various ways loved her, and really when you think about it that's a terrific compliment to her, that not one or two but *twelve* guys all thought she was the coolest thing since sliced bread, at least for a while, and in two cases, mine and Nine's, years at a time, not every woman could say that, eh?

This seemed like a good idea at the time but the next day I concluded it was nuts but unfortunately Nine did not forget about it and a few months later he called to tell me that he had tracked down four of the other boyfriends, all of whom lived within a hundred miles, and they were amenable to some sort of minor event, from sheer stupid male curiosity, so I made an effort and tracked down three of the old boyfriends myself, so that left three to find—the hockey player, the mustache guy, and the guy she went out with for about ten hours total over the course of four howling drunk days in Texas. This last guy turned out to be in Uruguay, and the friend of a friend of my wife's who told me where he was also pointed out in no uncertain terms that this boyfriend, I'll call him Seven, was a complete and utter ass and thief and snake of whom not enough words in the world could cover what a snake he was, so I concluded not to invite him, and Nine and I turned our efforts to finding One and Ten, and you would be surprised how easy it is to find somebody once you really put your mind to it, you wonder if maybe you should be a private detective on the side and make a little cash finding old boyfriends for various purposes, it's something to think about.

Anyway Nine found One, who turned out to be a professor of entrepreneurship at a community college, and I finally tracked down Ten, who turned out to be gay as a three-dollar bill and in a stable relationship finally and not at all interested in reviewing the past during which he had so strenuously tried to find his true identity, so Nine and I decided to go with the ten guys we had, and after talking about possible venues for a while we settled on a bus trip, you know, like an Outing, which would give us a chance to talk a bit but would not be so formal an arrangement as a dinner or anything, and neither Nine nor I thought that a weekend away made much sense, for one thing who had the money? and for another can you imagine explaining to your wife that you are forsaking her and the children for a weekend away with a bunch of guys you don't actually know and the only thing you have in common is that you have all kissed the same woman deep in the thickets of the past? I think not.

So we rented a bus for the day, a small bus, sort of half a bus, what my kids would call a little kid bus, and we hired a guy to take us out in the wine country for the day, and as we boarded the bus, grinning a little nervously, I remembered my grandfather telling stories about the outings he used to go on when he was a boy in Ireland, all the men and boys in his village would pile into an old lorry and go drinking for the day, even the boys would have a pint or two and get all sozzled, and the men would drink like heroes and warriors, and end up in the bushes, and everyone would tell hilarious stories the rest of the year until it was time for the outing again. It seemed like an odd custom when he told us about it, always with high glee and he would laugh so hard he would get short of breath and have to lie down, but as I boarded the bus with the boyfriends I saw how it could actually be a lot of fun, you would spend a lot of time just sitting with the other guys telling stories and jokes and it would be a grand day absolutely, as my grandfather liked to say.

Anyway we all got sozzled, the other nine boyfriends and me, and all day guys were ribbing me for having won her hand, I was elected president of the bus and got to make decisions about which wineries to stop at and all, and in the end it was sort of poignant, each guy had a whole subsequent life after dating my wife, and he would struggle to tell you about his life in short order, which is not easy to do, and each guy too said with genuine affection and respect that my wife was a wonderful woman absolutely, an unforgettable woman, that his time with her was really a highlight of his life and after they broke up he had kicked himself for some time about having lost such a princess of a woman, but life goes on, you know, and you meet other people, and there are blessings in sadness, and he would have never had the kids he had if he had not broken up with my wife and met his first or second wife, and things like that.

We ribbed the driver for not having gone out with my wife, and when people at the wineries asked politely what our group was we would lose it laughing and not be able to explain, and there were a lot of funny stories of all sorts, and we all agreed by voice vote on the way home that this had been a terrific thing we should do only the once for fear of losing the spontaneous zest of it, but what I will remember from the day isn't the laughter, of which there was a lot, which is a good thing, but a moment of silence on the way home when I am pretty sure that every guy on the bus, including the driver, was thinking about how you take certain forks in the road in your life, and one fork leads to another, and while this is totally natural and all, and we all accept it and even savor it, especially guys like me who somehow end up with the princess, isn't it strange how one decision going the other way would have put you into a whole different life, with a different wife and different kids and a different dog? We hardly ever think about this and there's no percentage in thinking about it but for a moment there on the bus every guy thought about it, and no one said anything for a while until Nine said hey, does she still change her mind every seven seconds or what? and that set us all laughing and telling stories again until we got back to the place where we had all left our cars. We got off the bus laughing like little kids and laughed harder when Seven dropped the bottle of wine he was taking home to his wife, it exploded with a terrific bang, and then we all shook hands and said goodbye and that was the end of that.

DO YOU THINK WE SHOULD PULL OVER?

Which famously was the question my friend Pete asked me as we were driving in New Hampshire and his car, this was the Datsun, BURST INTO FLAMES! FLAMES WERE SHOOTING FROM THE ENGINE RIGHT IN FRONT OF OUR EYES! and Pete asks hesitantly *do you think we should pull over?* as I am shrieking *pull over!!!!!!* and hammering on the dashboard hoping that indeed he will soon pull over so we can exit sprinting across the icy stubbled fields into the dense and brooding forest, from which refuge we watched the fire burn out eventually, and shuffled wearily back to the car, and stood there freezing and snarling until a guy came by and drove us into town in his truck, which had, no kidding, huge flames painted on it. We agreed that the flames on his car looked pretty cool.

Then there was the time we were driving, this was also in New Hampshire, you wonder what it is with Pete and cars and the Granite State, and THE FLOOR FELL OFF HIS CAR, in such a way that you could SEE THE HIGHWAY SPEEDING BY BELOW YOUR FEET, and I screamed that time too!!! and hammered my sneakers on the dashboard until he pulled over!! but that time he didn't ask me if he should pull over, he just pulled over, having learned his lesson. Pete points out that the *whole* floor didn't fall off the car that time, just most of the front part, and he notes also that it is *not* accurate to say, as I have said, that the *chassis* fell off, because the chassis did *not* fall off, only a vast piece of the floor, which apparently had rusted to dust because the car was ancient beyond reckoning, it may have been the first car ever invented, this was not unlikely, that car was probably four hundred years old, probably the conquistadores owned that car, and Pete had paid something like three hundred bucks for it, which is not the least he ever paid for a car, no no, not by a long shot, for there was the convertible he bought for a hundred dollars, this was the Impala, he drove *that* car THROUGH THE CAR WASH WITH THE TOP DOWN to see what it would feel like, which he said it felt great except that he lost his spectacles in the rush of water. That car, the Impala, never did dry out, although it dried out better than our friend Billy's car, this was the Chevy, which he parked near an ocean before a hurricane, and it drowned.

Pete actually bought another car for a dollar, this was the Buick, from a guy who said there were no dents, go ahead and walk around it and see if there are any dents, boys, which we did, and there was a huge dent on the right front side, and I said, fairly reasonably, I thought, hey, there's a huge dent over here, and the guy says to Pete, who's your asshole hippie freak friend? anyway Pete buys this car hurriedly, but it turns out the car was sensitive to weather, and whenever the temperature went up or down more than ten degrees overnight the car wouldn't work until the temperature went back to what it liked, which was about eighty, because the car had been born in Florida or something. One time we went to the movies, Pete and me, this was *To Have and Have Not*, directed by Howard Hawks, just a terrific movie, the rare kind of movie in which you want to live for a while, and a cold front blew in during the movie, and we had to PUSH THE CAR ALL THE WAY HOME, because we didn't have money for a taxi, and the buses didn't run after midnight, and you can't just *abandon* a car, as Pete said, it's your *car*, man, you have to be responsible for it, otherwise you shouldn't even *have* a car, am I right?

Another time he had a car, this was another Buick, which a dog got stuck to, this was a Labrador retriever named Hank, but the details of this story remain sketchy, as Pete says the dog was trying to MATE WITH THE CAR, which is highly unlikely, and Billy says the dog *froze* to the car, which is much more likely, because this was in Vermont, where it gets to be like eighty below although Vermonters don't admit this and go around wearing nothing but vests as if a *vest* would keep you warm, all a vest keeps warm is like your spleen or something, and Hank wasn't the brightest bulb in the galaxy, there are a *lot* of stories about Hank, but we are talking about cars. Although one time Pete strapped a hockey mask on Hank and sent him roaring among his little nieces and nephews at Christmas, which caused a memorable ruckus, and another time Hank got stuck to a train to Montreal, which was supposedly an accident, but you wonder.

Anyway the last story I wanted to tell you about Pete and cars was another car Pete bought for a dollar, this was the Volvo, which was also an ancient car, and which the seller had parked out in his back yard under some trees for about twenty years, but he had left a window open a few inches, so the car was really moist and funky inside, with slugs and moss and such, and a seedling, this was a maple, had TAKEN ROOT IN THE BACK SEAT and expanded to startling proportions. Pete went through this car meticulously after he bought it, finding about ten dollars in loose change but leaving the tree, because as he said it would be just wrong to kill a living thing, and he gave the car to his wife Colleen for Christmas, which always seemed a complicated gift, I mean, who wouldn't want a car for Christmas, but a car with a maple tree growing out of the back seat is not the kind of car you maybe pick out first for your girl if you were picking out cars for your girl, am I right?

2. YOU KNOW WHAT I'M SAYING?

The car that we estimated was easily four hundred years old, which may have been driven by the conquistadores, possibly when they fled the Yaqui people in the Sonoran desert, most of the Spanish warriors fleeing south, but three or four of them, says Pete, probably crowding into the car, which is just big enough to fit four guys with major armor and weaponry, and flooring it north to Kansas, well, *that* car, it was a Ford, of course, which Pete bought from a guy who had bought it in Kansas from a girl who said she bought it after a guy drove it into a river, it still had a *lance* in the trunk, and it's not like you find the working end of an old Spanish lance in the trunk of your car every day, you know what I'm saying?

A guy I know in Boston who knows weapons better than he should, says Pete, he says it's not a lance, it's the working end of a *halberd*, which is what conquistadores carried more than they carried lances, said this guy, because lances were mostly for guys on horses, which is why they were called lancers, whereas your regular guys who walked carried halberds, which were like axes seven feet long, you got to have some major forearms to swing those suckers, so what you got here in your car, says the guy to Pete, that is most definitely the business end of a halberd.

Not to mention, says Pete, that the maps in the car were really old and were *printed in Spanish*, that's a dead giveaway, and of course the conquistadores had *never been in Kansas before*, and of course they didn't know what road to take. I mean, think about it, you get lost on those little county roads there, the ones that wander aimlessly through farms and ranches because a hundred years ago the guy surveying the road wanted to survey the farmer's daughter, you could stay lost for a hundred years, because it's not like those roads have signs, you know what I'm saying? And you could go for years without seeing anyone to ask for directions, and when you do find someone, and ask for directions, the farmer maybe doesn't focus on directions because what he sees is four burly guys wearing major serious armor, with those helmets that look like the Sydney Opera House, and the grimy beards and all, probably their swords sticking out the back window, you know, his directions would be like *go to where the farmer's daughter used to live and turn right*, that kind of thing, very confusing.

And if the maps and the halberd are not enough, says Pete, here's the kicker: *there are no seat belts in the car*. Think about it. Seat belts were made mandatory by our government in the year

1600, when the French tried to steal America, so a car without seat belts must, ipso facto, be from *before* 1600. Also the radio *only gets Spanish stations*, and what does that tell you? It tells you that the car was Spanish, and the radio frequency sensor in the engine can only understand Spanish. You have to know something about cars when you are working with history stuff like this, says Pete, otherwise you end up just listening to any old nut saying any old thing. But the fact is that there are facts, which is what we are talking here, and then there is nutty stuff, which is why God invented talk radio, which the car *does not get*, and what does that tell you, you know what I'm saying?

3. THE GRIEF DIET

Anyway the last story I want to tell you about Pete and cars, well, this story isn't as funny as the other stories, but it matters that you know it, so here it is: One time he lived in his car for a while. It's not what you think, that he was homeless and desperately poor and had to live in a hulk parked in the woods where a guy abandoned it and blackberry brambles took over in that greedy possessive way they have, all snarling and prickly, and he had to dive dumpsters for old doughnuts and soda cans and such. No, this was during the Dark Year, the year of the eclipse, as he says, when the tide came in and covered him, and he went walkabout for a while.

This was hard on his wife and children, you bet, and even his dog was crushed, but Pete is that lucky kind of guy who his wife likes him even when she is furious and terrified and knows that there's nothing she can do for him, and his kids were teenagers and so maybe they didn't even *notice* he was gone for a while, although me personally I think they *did* notice and were just quietly praying like hell in the roiling temples of their hearts, and it's interesting to me that the dog went out hunting for Pete for days and days, one of the kids told me that, it would leave every morning and spend the whole day searching town and beach and woods for the big guy, coming home exhausted at night and sleeping by the door so that anyone who opened the door at night would hit the dog right in the kidneys, which the dog couldn't really afford, that dog peed every eleven seconds, pretty much.

Anyway we were talking about Pete living in his car, this was the Park Avenue, which is a really big car, Pete says there was plenty of room in the back seat where he hung his suits and everything, because he still went to work at the investment firm, he'd just take a shower at the gym in the morning and drink a lot of coffee, because as he says he was always really tired, that's the worst thing about the black dog, he says, you get *really tired*, no one ever tells you that part, you are just wiped out, you can't think straight, how come no one ever says *that* part, you read all this stuff about depression and chemical imbalance and midlife crisis and no one ever says really the worst thing is you feel like you could sleep for a week and you'd still feel like you hadn't slept since Lincoln was president, you know what I'm saying? Also I couldn't eat, and I lost twenty pounds. The grief diet, man.

Anyway Pete says if you have to sleep in your car for a while you could do a lot worse than a Park Avenue, and he had satellite radio too, and reclining heated seats, and he collected the newspapers every evening from the doughnut shop, and the policeman knew him and left him alone hoping, like everybody else, that things would change and Pete would make a comeback, which he did, finally, for no particular reason that he could explain except maybe that people kept leaving notes on his car, first it was people who knew him like his wife and kids and co-workers and neighbors, and then it was even people who *didn't* know him, schoolkids and truckers and people like that. Pete thinks maybe the cop, his name was Michael, quietly told everybody what was up, and suggested leaving notes under his windshield wipers like traffic tickets in all sorts of colors, and Pete says in the beginning he didn't have the gas to read the notes but then there got to be so many on the windshield that he couldn't actually *see* out the windshield, and he started reading them and enjoying them, some of them were so funny, and then people started leaving money under the windshield wipers, and maybe that was the thing that pushed me over, says Pete, you can't be taking money from people because you have the black dog, that's just bad *form*, man, so I went home, nailing the dog right in the kidneys with the door, I *told* that dog never to sleep there but he doesn't listen to me, and my wife and kids were real sweet about the whole thing, they didn't say much, they just hugged me and all, and my oldest kid says *what's with all the notes on your windshield?*, which cut the tension, so that was pretty much that. Had to take the dog to the vet later for some kidney problem that cost me a bundle, which I figured was my penalty fee for being on vacation from life, you know what I'm saying?

4. LESTER'S BEST DAY

But I'll tell you one more story about Pete, this time not about cars so much as the dogs who rode in his cars, for he had a long line of great crazy dogs, Hank and Mugga and Lester and Tommy, not to mention the time he briefly owned a pony because of a girl, but that's another story altogether, and we were talking about the dogs.

Lester, now, he was a really great dog, the kind of dog who could run all day, Pete would take him out to the pond and they would run *the whole pond*, which is like nine miles around, and Lester at the end of the run was fresh as a flower, not even panting hard, you wondered how far that dog actually *could* run, which is why Pete signed him up for the marathon one year, that was the year Pete ran the marathon wearing buffalo horns for some reason we can't remember now, the year he got all the way to the top of Heartbreak Hill, right near Boston College, that's like at twenty miles, and the president of the college was there among the spectators, easily discernible because of his collar, he is a priest, you know, and Pete stops and reaches into his jock and pulls out a soaking wet twenty dollar bill and says to the startled president here's a donation for the college, Faddah, don't spend it all in one place, and runs off down the hill toward the finish line with the poor priest standing there with the moist twenty, which god knows you wouldn't want to have *that* in your hand, you know what I mean?

Anyway we were talking about Lester, who got a number and everything, the race registrar wasn't paying attention or conspired with Pete, and Pete wanted Lester to run with sunglasses but Lester declined, and he wouldn't wear the official shirt either, although he did wear his number. He took off at the beginning of the race, not pacing himself at *all* despite what Pete had told him again and again about setting a steady pace, and by the fifteen mile mark he was drained. We found him long after the race, sleeping under a guy's car, and when Pete hauled him out, Lester complaining about his sleep being disturbed, one of the neighbors said Lester had committed An Incident with a female poodle and a child had been scandalized, so it wasn't, all in all, Lester's best day.

I should tell you about Hank and Mugga and Tommy, but there are just so many stories about Lester that once you get started telling stories about Lester there's no end to them at all, like the time he did win a ten mile race along the river by cutting in front of the leader at the very last second, this was after a heroic comeback on the last downhill stretch, he was just *flying* down that hill, Pete's theory is that Lester came about as close to the sound barrier in that last thousand yards as any dog ever has, which may be right, because I was there, at the finish line, waiting for Pete, and you couldn't even *see* Lester he was going so fast, he was like a blur rocketing along the road, a most amazing sight. He got his blurry picture in the paper the next day, and Pete bought him a steak.

There are a lot of other Lester stories, like the time he got married to Pete's cousin's boyfriend's dog The Little Death, *that* was a roaring party, and how he learned to surf, although he was terrible at it, and how he appeared in a short story by a famous writer, two of whose short stories were made into movies, but the guy never did seem to have any money even after the movies, and he still drove around town with a baseball bat in his trunk in case of trouble and a hundred bucks under the mat on the driver's side in case he got caught short. Famous as he was out in the world, he could still be found at the sub shop almost every day, ordering the steak bomb and ogling the waitress, and he still tried hitting on the other professors' daughters whenever he got the chance, which is scummy except in one case where the daughter was literally the most beautiful girl in the history of the universe, and she had an excellent dog, too, but that's another story.

5. KITTY'S BACK

I *swear* this is the last story I'll tell you about Pete and cars, and I suppose really it's a story about me, and why I love the big guy—not *that* way, but in the way you love a really dear friend who *gets* you and you *get* him and you have a million stories to choke with laughter over, the kind of guy who when you are driving with him and he snorts suddenly and says *remember that time we got stuck in the snow in Flagstaff?* you both start laughing so hard you have to pull over and wipe the water out of your eyes and wonder how come when you laugh really hard your cheeks and stomach ache, why is that? That kind of guy.

Anyway, we were sitting out behind a pub on the beach in New Hampshire in the convertible, this was the Impala that he drove through the car wash later with his bathing suit on and the top down, the Impala that never really did totally dry out after that, although Pete said it was *totally* worth driving through the car wash because, as he says, how often do you get to drive through a car wash with the top down, you know, which is an excellent question, and I am sprawled in the back seat, sipping beer, and he is in the front seat, fiddling with the tape deck, and the ragged convertible top is folded down, and it's a glorious warm starry summer night, you just cannot imagine a more lovely night in the United States of America, you can smell ocean and beer and fried dough, and faintly through the walls of the pub we can hear the bar band roaring through what sounds like the greatest hits of Southside Johnny and the Asbury Jukes, and there are girls laughing somewhere nearby, which is a terrific sound, and there's a piney breeze from the forest on the hill, and Pete says, *man, this is it, I found the legendary Kitty's Back tape,* which is the greatest mystery tape in the history of Bruce Springsteen bootleg tapes, a live tape that was supposedly recorded with unbelievable technical skill by a weird genius engineer in the summer of 1974 when Springsteen and the E Street Band had arrived at full intense throttle as a band, all their capacious skills at a peak, plus years of experience on the road, plus still they had wild youthful joy and exuberance, this was before they got so huge that you had to mortgage your house to get a ticket, and you couldn't get a ticket anyways because tickets were snapped up *before they went on sale* by stockbrokers and scalpers, and this tape, the famous Kitty's Back tape, was a shadowy legend, we were always meeting someone who had heard it or someone who knew someone who had it, but you couldn't buy it, of course, and every time you pursued it deliberately it would get lost, or a guy's cousin's tape deck had eaten it, or someone's mother accidentally poured battery acid on it, or something like that.

So when Pete held up the tape like a trophy, grinning like a whale, I sat up straight, and when he popped it in the tape deck and cranked it up large and the band tore into the song "Kitty's Back" I almost fainted, and believe me when I tell you the sound was clear and crisp and wild and clean and loud as if the band was perched on the deck of the Impala, and it went on for twenty howling minutes easy, the band building to an incredible pitch, and Pete got so excited he started jumping up and down in the front seat, and Pete is no pixie, so the car was shaking like a dog after a bath, and something about the moment just *nailed* me where I live down deep, you know?

I mean, you could talk about all the ingredients here, the stars and beer and summer and glorious extraordinarily American music, and the laughter of girls on the beach, and the smell of pine trees, and the fact that we were young and strong and stupid, and happy in a ratty old convertible, with no duties and responsibilities, yet, but there was something else at play, something I never forgot, something I savor, all these years later. I don't have any good words for it, even now, but there was a moment there, when Pete was leaping up and down in the front seat and I was jumping up and down in the back, and the car was shucking and jiving, and the music was so unbelievably loud and wild you couldn't imagine there had ever been a song so joyous and intense and thorough in the world before, and people walking by were laughing fit to bust, that I got as close to something as I ever got. I have been *happier*, sure, in far deeper ways, like the time I danced with my new astounding wife at our wedding reception, or when our startled children slid out of her years later with wet resounding plops, but there was something that night by the beach, something nutty and silly and electric, that makes me smile every time I think about it, which is pretty often. Maybe the silliest moments are actually the most important ones, you know? Or maybe moments like that are like windows that you drive by really fast, and just for an instant you see something crazy and cool, and then it's gone, and all you can do is grin and remember.

YODA

One summer day my neighbor to the one side tells me that the daughter of the neighbor to the other side is pregnant.

O, I say, and my heart goes right out to the daughter.

She's maybe sixteen, this kid, as sweet and gentle a girl as you'd ever want to meet. Quiet but quick and diligent around the house and yard. Smart as a whip. Takes classes at the community college already. A great kid. Not averse to helping me carry grocery bags or prune the fruit trees and such when she sees I am having trouble doing stuff now that I am old.

I don't see much of the daughter in the next few days, she stays inside the house, doesn't work in her garden like usual, and her boyfriend doesn't come around anymore.

It's not like I am especially close to this kid. I am not even fully sure of her name, which is either Laura or Laurie. I missed her name the first time she mentioned it, when she and her mom moved in next door a while ago, and when people talk about her they don't pronounce the ending of her name clearly enough for me, and now it's too late to just ask her name. I'd look like I am getting senile, and I am a little touchy about looking like I am getting senile, because I think maybe I *am* getting senile, so there you are.

I see her at the mailbox a couple of times in the next weeks, and one time I meet her by the mailbox, and she smiles and I smile, but neither of us says anything, and she hustles home with the mail.

She doesn't look too pregnant to me but what do I know.

Things go on this way for a while and by the holidays she swells up and there's no question she's pregnant. I watch her getting the mail. We all live on a steep hill and I see her working harder and harder to get back up the hill with the mail.

Pretty soon it's spring and I am out in the garden most of the day. I may be getting old and senile but the knees and back and arms still work pretty well and I like growing things. I take a certain pride in my garden, which is carefully plotted out and very productive. I have stuff growing there all year long. You can do that here because even though it rains all winter it never freezes, so I can keep turnips and potatoes and chard and kale going right through the winter. The rest of the year I have beans, blueberries, carrots, garlic, onions, peas, peppers, radishes, raspberries, rosemary, squashes, strawberries, tomatoes, and thyme. Along the fence between my house and the girl's house I have fruit—an apple tree, a pear, a fig, and some grapevines.

Pruning the trees and vines is where she's been a real help to me, because she was deft with those shears, and she was studying botany and stuff at the college, so she was actually interested in the way things grew and all, and it used to be that she was tireless, and one hour of her pruning was worth ten hours of me pruning because she was made of rubber and never got tired.

But now she's not made of rubber and one day when I am out there pruning she walks out slowly and leans on the fence and apologizes for not helping.

Hey, no problem, I say.

I feel like I let you down, she says.

No no, I say.

I'm not in a condition to be much help.

How you feeling? I say.

Heavy, she says.

When are you due? I say.

Good Friday, she says. Can you believe it? Of all the days to have a baby. That's the saddest darkest day of the year.

I am no particular religion but I know enough of the Christian thing to know what she's talking about.

Maybe you can keep the baby inside you for a couple days and give birth on Easter, I say.

That'd be something, she says.

That'd sure be something, I say.

I'll help you again when I'm in better shape, she says.

That'd be great, I say, and she walks slowly back to her house.

The older I get the less I sleep, and on Good Friday I am up before dawn. I make coffee and go out in the garden to watch the sun come up. There's a place there where the angle of the fence is such that no one in the houses or the street can see you.

As soon as I get to the fence, though, I notice loose dirt, and I get a bad feeling, and dig into the dirt and feel a tiny foot the size of my thumb, so I dig like crazy and get the baby out in about three seconds, it's all muddy but still breathing, I can tell from the tiny chest going up and down, so I stuff it in my shirt and walk quick into my house and wash it off in the sink and there I am with a baby the size of a bird.

I wrap it in a towel and it looks at me but it doesn't cry.

It's a boy.

I get all rattled for a little while there and have to sit down.

The thing is so little you wouldn't believe it. It's about as big as a cup of coffee. It looks like Yoda in those Star Wars movies, to tell you the truth.

I take it into the bedroom and lay it on the bed and wrap more towels around it because someplace I read that newborns get really cold really fast, which makes sense because they have been in the wet oven for a long time and being born must be an awful shock. Not to mention getting buried by the fence.

I don't know much about this all, because I never got married, and while I have a lot of nieces and nephews, and I really like kids, I don't really know anything about them technically. So I was in a pickle.

But men are not as stupid and helpless as movies and television shows make us out to be. I mean, I was in two wars, I worked in the woods, I live alone, I can figure things out, so we figured things out, Yoda and me. We figured out that he could suck hot milk off the end of a moist towel, which he really liked, and we figured out that he liked to sleep a lot, and we figured out that he slept best when I put him back in my shirt and rocked in the rocking chair. He really liked that. The only time he really cried like he meant it was when we got up out of the rocking chair. He didn't like that and he cried hard but he was so little that him crying hard wasn't much sound at all. I didn't tell him that because I didn't want to hurt his feelings, you know, but he sounded like a toy teapot. Plus as soon as he commenced to cry I gave him the milk towel again and that was that. He sure liked that milk towel.

Friday went by right quick, Yoda and me sleeping that night in the rocking chair, and Saturday was dusking by the time I made up my mind what to do.

We spent another night in the rocking chair, Yoda and me, and then before dawn I gave him another bath in the sink, which he liked, and wrapped him up tight in a towel, and gave him a huge dose of the milk towel, which knocked him out cold, and then I watched out the window for the girl next door getting the Sunday newspaper.

Soon as she went by my house, walking gingerly, I whipped out to the fence with Yoda in my shirt and waited on her. When she came back up the hill she came over to the fence to say hi and I worked her over to the place where the angle of the fence is such that no one in the houses or the street can see you and I pulled old Yoda out of my shirt.

Look what I found, I say.

She doesn't say anything but her eyes are all wild.

He really likes sucking hot milk off a towel, I say.

She doesn't say anything.

And he likes warm baths, I say.

She reaches over the fence for him and I hand him over and she pulls him in to her chest with a sound in her throat you couldn't describe if you had a year.

Thank you, she says very quiet.

No problem, I say, very quiet.

We stand there for a minute, all three of us, and then she goes back to her house with Yoda and I pretend to examine the grape-vines in case her mom is watching and then I go make some coffee and come back out and sit by the fence and watch the sun come up full power. Then I get back to work in the garden because there is an awful lot to be done and spring is most definitely sprung.

THE CUCKOLD 10K

I came home early from work one day and found my wife Shari in bed with a guy. All I saw was a tangle of pink bodies in the bed. I recognized Shari's feet. Our son Donnie was in his playpen in the living room. I don't know who the guy was. Donnie just turned a year old and is just starting to walk—you know how when kids start to walk they hold onto the furniture and scuttle along sideways and occasionally make a tentative foray out into the middle of the room? That's where Donnie is. It's a sweet time.

I wanted to get away from this scene as quickly as possible but what do I do with Donnie? He was facing the other way and didn't see me which was good, because otherwise he would have shouted *dadda* and things would get complex.

I was standing in the hallway by the coats and I had this powerful urge to just cover myself with the coats for a few months.

I go softly back through the kitchen and back out the door and back into the car and back on the road. Drove until dark, which is when I usually come home, and then I went home, and Donnie shouted *dadda* and Shari was there making chicken with garlic and rice. We had dinner. I opened a good bottle of white, as it seemed like kind of an occasion. We puttered around putting Donnie to bed and then I did the laundry and Shari got the upstairs room ready for visitors. Some college friends are coming Friday for the weekend, driving up from Phoenix.

I kind of just wanted to have a quiet night at home.

Yesterday I went to work and came home at the regular time and we had steak. I opened a good bottle of red—a zinfandel, figuring that would go well with the meat—and Shari said *what's the occasion?* And right there I should have said something but I just wanted to have a sweet quiet night, so I just said *life's short*, and she grinned.

Things went on like that for a while—I didn't say anything and she didn't say anything and I made sure I didn't come home early from work anymore. Things were a little awkward in bed but I just said I was tired from work.

It was actually a nice time. Just to have dinner, and play with Donnie, and play chess or read with Shari as the rain rattled the windows, that seemed like heaven to me—warm and quiet and peaceful. No one yelling.

You know how when someone cheats on someone in the movies or in a book it's dramatic when they get caught, and there's a wild scene? I think that's made up. I bet most of the time when the guy or the woman realizes what's happening, they just get sad. I think most of the people who get cheated on just take it and try to figure out what to do next. What else are you going to do? Leave your life?

The thing is, I really *like* Shari—she's funny and sweet and sexy and being with her has been the best thing in my life before Donnie. Now I feel different about her, sure, but still we have our life.

Another month went by like this and I spent a lot of time running and playing basketball. I tried to think while working out so I could think clearly and not lose my temper. I recommend it for people who are upset about something.

One night I was running and I caught up to a guy ahead of me and fell into pace with him. You do this sometimes when running—you just end up running with someone you don't know. It's like playing a foursome in golf with guys you don't know.

We ran up Pill Hill and stopped at the top to stretch and catch our breath and we got to talking about running. I was saying how

I felt running was a great way to burn off confusion and pain and he says he agrees, in fact he runs every night to deal with his wife screwing one of his friends.

This was pretty amazing. I tell him about Shari and he says he knows another guy in the same position and that he's a runner too. So the next night we all three ran together, five miles, stopping again on Pill Hill to talk.

A week later another guy joined us, a friend of his, and we got to running every other night, five miles. We'd go once around town and then up Pill Hill as hard as we could go and then stop on top for a while and stretch and talk and then run down and home to our warm houses with our cheating wives.

One night a cop swings by as we are stretching and talking on Pill Hill. He wants to know what's up—he's had a complaint from a neighbor that men are gathering at night in the park. Complainant thought it was a coven of warlocks. We explain that we're just guys with a shared problem and it turns out that *he* came home two weeks ago to find his wife in bed with his brother. He beat them both up and has been living in a motel since but he says doesn't know what to do now.

Unfortunately he's not a runner but he says it's time for him to get into shape and so he starts running with us, too, although it takes him more than a month before he can make it up Pill Hill. He gets suspended from the force for two weeks in there for beating up his brother and wife, and he uses the time off to run.

Meanwhile he brings another cop into the group and then a fireman hears about it and joins. We had to laugh that night. I mean, seven cuckolds running through town, it was hilarious. It was like the punchline to a joke.

Then one night when we got to the hill there was a young woman waiting. She was in running gear and was stretching. Turns out she'd heard about the cuckold run and wants to join. I explain that we all have a certain problem in common and she says she has the same problem—her husband is a principal and he was screwing not one but two of his teachers, kindergarten and seventh grade. So she joins us, and a week later she brings a friend, and after a while she brings the boyfriend of the kindergarten teacher.

Now we have a real good crowd running every night. We keep that same crowd through spring and into early summer. By the beginning of June it's light on the hill and we see faces clearly, all my fellow cuckolds—young and old, fat and thin, bubbly and quiet. One night a guy announces that his wife just had a baby and he passes around little special water bottles shaped like cigars. No one asks if he's the father.

That night one of the older guys asks what everyone's doing for the summer. Turns out a lot of us are going on long vacations, some alone, some just with their children and not the cheating spouse, some with their wives and children. The principal's wife says she's planning a vacation just with her husband to try to keep their marriage going.

Before we break up for the summer, says the first cop, let's have one last run. How about June 21—longest day of the year?

How about a race? one guy asks.

Yeh—the Cuckold 10K, says one of the women.

We all laugh and agree to do it.

When I get home, Shari's making stir fry beef, which Donnie loves, I think because he can handle everything with a fork. I pick out a good bottle of nebbiolo and we have a good night. I want to say something about the race, about coming home to find her tangled naked with another guy, about how I want to find and kill the guy, about how I want to throw the wine in her face, but it's a warm quiet night, and I like her so much, and there's Donnie walking around now with that drunken-sailor swagger that little kids have, and I don't say anything. What's to say, really?

It's hard for people to keep quiet about something that excites them, and the Cuckold 10K is exciting for us, I guess, because news of it gets out, and the night of the race I see people along the road—lined up and craning their necks to see the runners like at a real race, or a parade. Right from the start of the race there are people along the way. Friends and families, I guess.

I don't think about the implications of this for a while. For the first mile I am trying to get my rhythm and breathing right and for the second mile I am trying to figure out where everyone is and how they are running. There are people ahead of me but two of them are the cops, running together for brotherhood, and they are fading. The two women are also running together and they look strong. Ahead of them a ways is the fireman and in front is the boyfriend of the kindergarten teacher. This guy is young and lean and he just flows over the road. He has real long hair that floats out behind him.

I figure I can catch the cops in the next mile, catch the women by the end, when we are going up Pill Hill, and that leaves the fireman and the young guy. So I should medal if I stay calm and attack the hill at the end.

At the three-mile mark there's a big knot of people waiting, some of them holding out cups of water, and I suddenly realize that if there are a lot of people watching the race that means a lot of people know we are cuckolds—probably that's *why* there are a lot of people watching the race, to see whose wife or husband or boyfriend is screwing around on them. We are like a running gossip column.

Right after that I pass the cops, and in the next mile I pass the fireman, and now with two miles to go I have the women right in front of me. They're so slight and lovely, these women—both of them beautiful and kind-hearted, as far as I could tell. How could a guy dick around on them?

I pass them just as the hill begins and now it's the boyfriend alone in front of me. I have to admire his form—he's made to run, runs like a deer, feet hardly touching the ground, big long strides, thin legs, a thin guy, no weight to carry. He pulls away from me even going uphill. This guy's terrific.

Near the top I see Donnie by the side of the road and when he sees me he starts to run too and falls down, right on his face, the poor kid. I slow down to pick him up but then I see Shari reach down and pick him up. She straightens up holding him and looks right at me and I think about stopping and having it all out right there, but here come the two women neck and neck so I pick up speed and finish the race behind only the young guy. The two women finish together holding hands.

After everyone finished we all shook hands and the first three finishers got medals that the fireman had cast in his machine shop. The two women took turns wearing their bronze medal. We all posed together for a photograph, and then the two women posed together with the bronze medal looped around both their necks.

Then just for fun we all ran back down the hill together, all of us runners, and at the bottom of the hill we split up, some walking home and others waiting patiently for the people on the hill.

THREE BASKETBALL STORIES

LEFTY

I played in a basketball league once in Boston that was so tough that when guys drove to the hole they lost fingers. One time a guy drove to the hole and got hit so hard his right arm fell off, but he was a lefty and hit both free throws before going to the bench. I heard later that he was furious he got taken out because his shot was really falling that night, and also I heard that his team later had a funeral for the arm with everyone carrying the casket with only one arm as a goof but they all got so howling drunk that they lost the arm and had to bury the casket empty and then they spent the rest of the night trying to remember every lefty guy in the history of sports which is way harder than you think.

There were all kinds of guys in that league. One team had a guy who had been in a pro football camp but they decided he was too crazy for pro football, can you imagine? Another team had a guy about six foot twenty but he was awful and we beat them by ten. There were all kinds of guys. One time a brawl broke out before the game even started and it took like twenty minutes just to shoot all the technicals and half the guys were thrown out before the game even started, which led one guy to argue metaphysics with the refs, you know, like how can you be thrown out of a game if there's no game yet? They threw him out too.

There were a lot of guys in that league who were unbelievable ballplayers but they all had some flaw, you know? Like they couldn't go left at *all*, or could do everything except score, or couldn't do anything *except* score, or lost their minds when the sun went down or whatever. A lot of guys were total horses on the court but total donkeys off it, you know? Every team had a couple guys like that. We had two, our center who was a terrific ballplayer but who sold dope at halftime and ended up going into real estate and a guard who we never knew if he would show up or not or even stay for the whole game, sometimes he wandered off at halftime and that was the end of him for the night. He was the nicest guy you ever saw. We didn't know where he lived or if he had a job or what. We just told him when the next game was and hoped for the best. Some guys thought he lived somewhere in the park where we played summer league but I don't know about that.

There was one team where everyone except one guy had lost their drivers' licenses so the one guy, he was the point guard, had to drive the whole team and finally he got so tired of driving everyone he quit and without him they lost four straight and missed the playoffs. Another team used to pull up in the parking lot in a huge garbage truck which one of their guys drove for work, you could hear them coming miles away, but only four guys could fit in the cab so six guys had to hang onto the back. Guys drove all sorts of things in that league, old buses and mail vans and such. One time a guy drove up in a Bentley but it turned out he stole it and he missed the rest of the summer though he was back for winter league.

Mostly we played for fun and to try to talk to the girls who came to watch the other teams. In summer they would sit up on the little hill above the court under the pines and sometimes we would call time out to get a look at them without the other team getting all wiggly the way they did if you wandered up there at halftime. You never knew if they were wives or girlfriends or sisters or what. One theory was that the girls who cursed the refs were girlfriends showing off, because wives and sisters could care less, but I don't know about that. One girl was the tallest girl you ever saw, she was taller than any of us, and there was another girl who wore a smile and not much else, we lost every game we ever played those guys, you wonder why.

Anyway, the guy who lost his arm, the story was that they finally found it again after the funeral for it and he ended up leaving it in a toll booth on the highway, with a quarter clenched in the fist, because rigor mortis set in, so the story was he paid a toll with it, but I don't know if that's true, although the guy who told me that was his teammate, the same guy who told me about the funeral for the arm, but this guy, the teammate, he and I got so absorbed in lefty talk that we never got into how true was the arm and the toll booth story, because the lefty thing is really interesting when you stop and think about it, Lefty Grove and Lefty Gomez and Sandy Koufax and Babe Ruth and Ted Williams were all lefties, and Bill Russell was lefty, and this guy, the teammate, claimed that Pele the great soccer player was lefty, although I said how would you know he's lefty if you can't use your hands in soccer, which he said that's a good point, but the clincher here is that the greatest middleweight boxer *ever* is lefty, Marvelous Marvin Hagler, and Marvin is from *Boston*, so there you go.

YO JOHN

One time I played on a summer team where I was the only white guy. This was in New York City a long time ago. There were nine other guys on my team and right from the start they couldn't remember my name no matter what and finally one guy, he was our center, he said all you white guys look alike to me, we'll call you John Lennon cause he have long hair and ratshit beard too, and they all laughed and said Yo John Lennon!

This didn't last too long because it's too long to be yelled when you want the ball which they all did all the time so my name got pruned down quick to Yo John and finally just to Yo, so I went a whole summer once being called Yo two nights a week all over New York City. I remember one night the ref asked me if I was Chinese or what and my team laughed so hard one guy hurt his ribs and had to miss a game.

There were some interesting guys on that team. One guy carried a shotgun in his trunk and twice carried it from the car to our bench to be sure everyone knew he was armored, as he said. We all scooted down the bench away from the gun. Another guy had tattoos over his entire torso front and back and when I asked him why he had none on his face he said Yo John, that's sick man, who would needle up his face?

We played all over the city. On one court in Bedford-Stuyvesant three men swept the broken glass off the court before the game began, all three in tandem with those long push brooms, like synchronized sweeping. Another court, in Harlem, after both teams entered the refs padlocked the gate from inside and the spectators hung their fingers in the fence. The rumor was Connie Hawkins was coming that night, he knew a guy who knew a guy, and I was wearing his number that summer, 42, so the guys on my team thought this juxtaposition was hilarious, Yo John be Connie Hawkins tonight, Yo John be mad dunking and all, you the man, Yo John! We lost by ten and Connie Hawkins didn't show and I played awful.

We won most of our games, including one wild game in Long Beach in the windiest conditions ever, you had to account for the howling wind even on free throws, there was sand drifting across the court during the game, and high above the shrill haunted music of nighthawks, and after our last game, in Queens, we stood around talking for a while. The guy with tattoos, he was going to the police academy in the fall, and our center was going to community college to play ball. The guy with the shotgun was going into the small business, as he said. The point guard wanted to open a bakery, that was his great dream, he said, if any of us were in Long Island City, man, you come by and I will take care of you, man.

Summer league teams are hatched in a hurry and dissolve without ceremony so I didn't expect to see those guys again but that Christmas I was playing pickup at a park in the city when three of those guys came by and stopped to talk. We shot the breeze and then they said Yo John, we saw your man John Lennon shot dead couple weeks ago and we are sorry, man, he was a good guy, those songs and all, he had a baby boy too. Cold to kill that man, Yo John. Crazy cold. We thought of you, man. Next summer we change your name, man. We call you Yo Connie Hawkins maybe, freak out the crowd, you know, a skinny whitey Hawk, other team laugh so hard we win by thirty every night, what you say to that, man, you in?

IN THE EQUIPMENT SHED AT THE PARK IN CHICAGO IN JULY IN AN UNBELIEVABLE HOWLING THUNDERSTORM

One time I was playing basketball with a bunch of guys from the Latin Kings and the Latin Eagles, those are street gangs in north Chicago, when the most unbelievable howling thunderstorm fell on us and everyone ran for the equipment shed, which was a ratty little aluminum shack in the middle of the park. It was filled with softballs and dodgeballs and rakes and dust and spiderwebs and bases with the stuffing coming out of the holes and softball bats with chips in them big enough so you couldn't use them in a game but you couldn't throw them away either because who throws away a perfectly good bat, you never throw away a bat that's not *all* the way cracked even if you are never going to use it again which is why there are probably like ten million bats in basements all over the world, which is kind of interesting when you think about it.

Anyway everyone crammed into the shed and there were so many guys and so little room that the five guys closest to the door had to let their shoulders get rained on. One guy lit a purple joint the size of his thumb and passed it around and everyone started talking and telling stories. It was raining so loud you could hardly hear, and they were all talking at once in Spanish and English, and it got pretty smoky pretty fast, but it was that unbelievable late summer rain, you know, like a hot ocean falling in a hurry, and if you went out in it you would be totally soaked in two seconds, so we waited.

Raining like a million elephants pissing, said one guy, and everybody laughed.

When the joint came around to me I said nah and the guy next to me looked peeved and I said can't play baked and he laughed and said can't play not baked, man, which led to a huge discussion about whether hoop was better stoned or straight. One guy said it took the edge off and another guy said it made you see everything better and another guy said it made you jump higher and I said nah you just *think* you jump higher whereas actually you float around totally useless, and they all laughed.

It seemed weird to have guys from two opposing gangs crammed together in the shed but first off it was raining like you wouldn't believe and secondly a guy told me the rule in the street was that a park could be shared under certain circumstances which these were but schoolyards could not be shared under any circumstances, they were sole territories for reasons having to do I think with children, which led to a huge discussion about boundaries and territories, which made me a little nervous because what if they started arguing about boundaries but they didn't.

Maybe it was the smoke or whatever but both gangs started remembering guys they knew, first great ballplayers who got shot or went to jail, and then guys who weren't good ballplayers but thought they were, and then guys who thought they were tough but weren't, and then guys who *were* tough but never talked about it, and guys who could always get girls but you couldn't figure out why, and that led to a *huge* discussion about girls, and how you could never truly figure them out, everything you thought you learned from one didn't apply to any of the others, even in the littlest tiniest things, and how usually the way it worked was that you could never get the girl you wanted but you could get the girl you didn't want, which as one guy said maybe that was the key, to *not* want the girl you wanted, but another guy said no no, the key to getting the girl you wanted was to *not* get the girl you *didn't* want, but by then we were all confused and the rain stopped and we emerged, blinking in the light.

Maybe it was the smoke but I remember that everything shone, the steaming asphalt, the jeweled nets hanging from the rims, the gleaming backboards, even the ball glowing brilliant orange. We split up into wet guys and dry guys and played the rest of the afternoon and by the time I walked home the streets were so dry you couldn't believe it had ever rained at all.

STAY FLUSH

In December of 1961 I was a bartender at a golf club in Palm Beach. One day a guy comes in and orders a whiskey. This was at noon. He was an older guy, maybe seventy. His tee time was at four but he said he was having a bad day and wanted to settle his nerves before he went out on the course.

Don't feel well, sir? I ask.

Afflicted by memory, he says, sipping.

Yes, sir.

Burdened is perhaps the better word, he says.

Can I be of assistance, sir?

No, thank you, he says. Another whiskey, please.

I get another whiskey for him and he stares out at the course for a while and then says, You know what, son, maybe you can help me. This will sound odd but it would help me a great deal if you would accompany me outside and just sit on the veranda and listen to me for a while. I have something to say. A cathartic impulse, as it were. A peculiar urge of the aged. A shriving, one might say. Do I need to talk to your manager or something? I am the guest of a member here and I might characterize this as an unusual guest service. I would be happy to make it worth your while and recompense the club suitably also. I am a man of some means. I know this sounds odd but I would be very grateful for a willing ear. What's your name?

Jack, sir.

Jack, he says, blinking. Jack. Well, Jack, to whom do I speak in order to request the pleasure of your company on the veranda?

My manager is Mr. Dineen, sir. In the restaurant.

The guy goes to the restaurant and I top off the rest of the drinkers at the bar. He and Mr. Dineen come back in a minute and Mr. Dineen says it's okay with him if I accompany our guest to the veranda for a conversation on cabbages and kings, whereas our policy here at the club is that the guest of a member is essentially himself a member in good standing for the duration of his visit, and he, Mr. Dineen, cannot imagine that I will not welcome a brief respite from my labors as a purveyor of spirits, and he, Mr. Dineen, sees no clear reason why I cannot spend time in our guest's company up to and until such time as our guest's foursome is ready to commence defeating the course, which is playing beautifully today, sir, very little wind, the greens a touch fast, and I remind you that the tees on eleven have been moved back a tad as a sign of respect for the increasing musculature of American manhood, long may we wave.

The guy thanks Mr. Dineen and they have a cash handshake and he and I step out on the veranda.

Let us savor the brilliant and miraculous light, such a gift in winter, he says, and we take a table in the sun and he stretches out his legs and starts talking.

I am seventy-three years old, Jack, he says. I am a man of some means. I have been blessed by nine children and have suffered the loss of three, leaving me six, many of whom have risen to prominence in the affairs of state and nation. I have committed sins, several of which I regret. I have served my nation and my family with all the energy and diligence I could muster. I feel that my time is coming to a close and I wish to be clear about some things before I go. I am choosing you as witness, Jack. *Finné,* in the Irish, he who hears what is spoken from the heart. An old Irish custom, to choose a stranger and to him issue a final testament. Honesty being easier to inflict on a stranger. With those we love we must be more circumspect, eh? In the old days this would be done on a holy mountain. But here we are on the veranda of a golf course. How very American. Are you Irish?

My grandparents were from Mayo, sir.

Mayo God help us, he says. My people were from Wexford. They fled the famine. As did my wife's people. They were from Limerick. Very poor people they were, too, God rest them.

Yes, sir.

So we are observing the tradition of millennia here, Jack. I am the teller of tales and you are witness to their telling. I hand over my stories and you receive them. There is a grave moral responsibility here, Jack.

Yes, sir.

For which I will recompense you handsomely, this being America.

Yes, sir.

So then. The facts are only bones. I was born in 1888. I was born in Boston. I was nominally educated at Harvard. I wanted to make money so badly I can still taste the tang of ambition in my mouth. I did whatever I could. I regret nothing in that arena. We lie and cheat and call it commerce. I ran banks, theaters, films, liquor, the buying and selling of influence. I was induced to enter the government, having become wealthy enough to attract the attention of the master thieves who have long manipulated the civic apparatus. I served as this and that. I was for a time the national agent of American interests in the heart of the very empire that had enslaved and starved our ancestors for centuries on end. The irony remains delicious. Yet my dream even when young was for my sons to surpass me. Also very Irish, no? You want to create a world in which your sons flourish. The final duty of the *taoiseach*, the chieftain. Daughters married, sons admired. And this has come to pass. One son on the very top rung, the other two much respected, my beautiful and vibrant daughters married.

Nine children, you say, sir?

Originally, he says, sipping.

I'm sorry, sir. How many are alive?

Six, he says. One son dead in a plane. One daughter dead in a plane. Another daughter dead to the world.

Sir?

She vanished. Her mind went. Her mind was taken. I allowed it to be taken. I did not tell my wife. I spoke of it to no one. She was flawed. She was not herself. I said yes to the operation. I gave my blessing. They said it would work. It didn't work. Not at all. Ruination. Despair. But she is safe now. A hospital, a nunnery, people wear white. I went there once. It's very quiet. Restful. A kind of limbo. She didn't know me. We do not speak of her. We do not use her name. I allowed her to be taken. We do not speak of her. Another whiskey, please.

I got him another whiskey.

Also I have not been a good husband, he says when I return to the table. It is what it is. I admire and respect my wife. She is a remarkable woman. I love her very much. Yet I have not been a good husband. It is what it is. I regret having caused her pain. I regret that very much. We do not speak of it.

Yes, sir.

So many other stories I could tell, Jack, he says, sipping. So very many. Shadows and illusions, gambles and adventures, drama and melodrama. I have sailed long in the world and studied people closely. Yet a man is measured really by his children, don't you think? Maybe that too is an Irish belief. But I don't think so. At the last, the end of the suffering road, in every culture, you are your children. They carry you inside them into the future. It is the nature of things. Your energy goes into theirs. It is how it is. The cycle of life. In a sense the child consumes the parent. You die so that they might live. The very essence of the Catholic idea, of course. The Eucharist, the miraculous food. So the death of a child before a father or mother is unnatural, a hole in the fabric, a savage wound. You never recover from the death of your child. You readjust your mask, you proceed onward, but your wound cannot heal. Your heart is pierced. The stigmata.

Yes, sir.

I will speak then of three wounds, Jack. I say them aloud as penance. My daughter who is dead to the world, my daughter who fell from the sky, my son who vanished over the ocean.

Yes, sir.

Of my daughters I can hardly speak. We do not speak of them. The one in white now, lost. The other falling from the sky over England when her plane hit a mountain. I had to identify her body. She was so peaceful. I wept for weeks. We did not speak of it.

And your son, sir?

Well, Jack, there's the story. He was the child of my heart, firstborn, riveting, marked for greatness. He was the chosen one. Not only by me. Also by God. I know this to be true. God chose that boy to be among the elect, to be a king. But there was a war. In the conduct of the war he died. Without the war he would be alive. Wars are human constructs, Jack. I worked against the war. I saw it for what it was, thievery on the grandest scale. There are always ways around wars. Outwit the thieves. But it burst out like a disease and took my son. He was the one, Jack. I know this to be true.

Yes, sir.

He was a Navy pilot, Jack. His plane exploded. The plane was crammed with explosives. He was to aim the plane at a Nazi rocket base in France and then bail out. The target village was Mimoyecques. I cannot forget the name. He was twenty-nine years old. He and his friend Bud took off at 5.55 in the afternoon and vanished at 6.20. His last words were Navy code: *stay flush*, he said into his radio set, and pulled the safety pin on the bomb load, and prepared to eject, and then the plane exploded with such force that only shards and splinters of it were ever found. The pilot in a companion plane nearby said he never saw such an explosion before or since. No bodies were ever found. Not a tooth, not a button. I had people comb the area for months for pieces of my son. Professional searchers. I am a man of means. They searched the village, hills, woods, beach. Divers searched the ocean. They found nothing. Not a hair, not a shred.

I'm very sorry, sir.

Thank you, Jack.

God rest him, sir.

Yes.

Another whiskey, sir?

No, thank you, Jack.

A terrible blow, sir.

We received a telegram from the Navy the next morning. Regret to inform you. My poor wife sobbing. It is what it is. The children sobbing. I went to my study. A brilliant morning like this one. I locked the door. I was in there for several days. I did not eat. They knocked, they wept in the hallway, they remonstrated with me, begged, slid notes under the door. Their notes curled and yellowed in the August heat. I still hear them sobbing in the hall sometimes. I played music to drown their cries. *Stay flush,* he said into his radio set. I have pored over those words, Jack. *Stay flush.* A koan, as the pagans say. Lost. He was the first. Then my two daughters lost. Each one torn from me as you would tear off a limb. So I am no longer a man. I am reduced and shriveled, legless, one arm left to shake my fist at the Lord. My time is ending. It is what it is. I know this to be true. I have called you to witness, Jack, and I have said the final words. *Finis, finné.* Three wounds were inflicted upon me and they will not heal. I accept them. I pay for my sins with the lives of my children. I cannot bear that burden any longer. I still hear them talking sometimes. I drown their cries with music. My first son, my first daughter, my second daughter. I killed them. I did not protect them and so I must die. It is what it is.

He sat silently for a few more minutes, looking out at the course, and I couldn't think of anything sensible or courteous to say.

After a while he stood up and smiled and shook my hand and said he was very grateful indeed for my courtesy to him and he would leave a little something for me with Mr. Dineen for my troubles. I said thank you and he said he really had better be getting to the locker room to meet his friends because when you were older it took longer to gird for battle, so to speak, and I said yes sir and we shook hands again and that was the last I saw of him.

Probably you know the rest of the story, that he was on the eleventh fairway after a good drive from the new tee placement when he had a huge stroke and had to be carried off the course, paralyzed. He spent the next eight years in his study in a wheelchair, unable to move or speak except for two words, *no* and *shit*. During those years two more of his sons were shot to death so he ended up with one son and four daughters alive from the original nine children.

The daughter in the nunnery died a year ago at age eighty-six, I saw in the paper. She liked to sing and write letters to her family. Sometimes she would write letters all day and night in a kind of frenzy. She sent letters to all her sisters and brothers whether they were alive or not. The family kept telling her that the one sister and eventually three of the brothers were dead so she shouldn't write letters to them anymore but she kept right on writing her letters to her family whether they were alive or not. The one person that she stopped writing to when he died was her dad. No one knows how many letters she wrote him over the years, or if he ever wrote her back, because he had all his correspondence destroyed after his stroke, and the nunnery burns letters to deceased patients as a matter of policy, but I like to think that maybe he did write her back, you know? If only for the two of them to try to figure out what her brother meant when he said *stay flush* into his radio set in the last seconds before he vanished into the air over the endless hungry sea.

BLUE

Blue was the regiment drunk. He looked just like W.C. Fields with the big red nose and everything. He was useless but he was the sweetest guy, not a mean bone in his body. He was just a drunk, is all. Drunk morning noon and night. Drunk from the minute he opened his eyes until the minute he shut them. The Army took everyone then.

One time we went out on a mission on our gunboats and when we got pretty deep into the bay we discovered our compasses didn't work. They were skewing all over the place. We thought it was some kind of magnetism thing but then we figured out they'd been drained. Compasses then were built so the needle floated on a little sea of alcohol. Blue had been sentry for the second shift and he carefully opened each one and drank the juice and then put them back together.

We sat there in the dark for a minute, no one talking.

Get Blue over here, says the lieutenant.

Blue gets hustled over from another boat. He's drunk.

Bristol, says the lieutenant. You drank the alcohol from the compasses.

Yes, sir, says Blue.

Putting the regiment in danger.

Yes, sir.

That's a crime, Bristol.

Blue doesn't say anything.

That's jail time, Bristol.

Blue doesn't say anything.

Treachery, Bristol.

We all sit there silent for a minute and there's no sound except the lap lap lap of the little waves against the boats.

We should move, sir, says Mahon.

In a minute, Mahon, says the lieutenant, and something in the way he says it makes us realize what's happening. He's had enough. Blue has stolen food and gas for booze, he traded his rifle for booze, he stole a truck and traded it for booze. He went AWOL and caused a wreck and he was the reason Gabe got shot at Ormoc.

I should shoot you in the head, Bristol, says the lieutenant.

Blue smiles, a little confused and a lot drunk.

Or leave you in the bay, says the lieutenant.

He'd make noise, sir, says Mahon.

Not if I shoot him in the head first, says the lieutenant.

We all sit there for another minute listening to the lap lap lap of the little waves.

I don't think the gunshot is a good idea, sir, says Mahon.

I'm sorry, sir, says Blue, sensing something bad.

Tie him to the gunwale, head down, says the lieutenant.

Sir? says Mahon.

He can drink all he wants with his head in the water, says the lieutenant.

Mahon and I are the nearest to Blue and we have no choice but to hang him over the side of my boat and tie him to the gunwale. Blue's sobering a little now but he's not sober enough to fight back and he hangs over the side like a dead dog. The top of his head is in the water and as soon as the boat starts up he'll drown if the bucking of the boat doesn't smash his brains out.

Mahon and I straighten up and wait for what's next.

Hey, you guys, says Blue faintly.

Back to base, says the lieutenant.

He'll drown, says Mahon quietly.

That's the idea, Mahon.

That's murder, sir, says Mahon.

No, Mahon, says the lieutenant. It's the punishment he deserves. When we get back to base he goes to jail.

He'll die on the way, says Mahon.

People die, Mahon, says the lieutenant.

This is murder, sir, says Mahon.

Mahon, you are relieved of duty. Get in Gabe's boat.

Mahon has no choice but to get in Gabe's boat. The lieutenant goes back to his boat. Each boat has two men, a gunner and a pilot, both of whom are also mechanics too. Mahon is my gunner. Blue is supposedly a gunner but he's never fired a gun and no one would let him near the pilot's seat. Mostly when we were going somewhere he just sat in the bow and held on. He had sea legs, I give him that—maybe because they were so rubbery. But he never got sick or anything.

He was getting sick now, though, all over himself, either from fear or from hanging upside down drunk with his head in the water.

If you stop your boat, says the lieutenant to me, you go to jail. Do you understand me?

Yes, sir, I said.

Back to base, said the lieutenant, and all the boats started up and swung around to follow Gabe, who had a pocket compass he always carried no matter what. It was a gift from his father who had been in the Army in the first war and was real proud of his son in the second war. I heard his father nearly went crazy when Gabe got shot at Ormoc.

I didn't know what to do so I started the engine too and swung around. Blue was yelling but the little waves were gagging him. I could hear the lap lap lap from where I sat and the sound he made when he tried to catch his breath between the little waves.

I should explain that we were Army, not Navy, even though we spent all our time in boats. We were the 592nd Engineer Boat and Shore Regiment of the Army's Boat Battalion. No one remembers now that the Army had a boat battalion, but there were a lot of us in the Pacific, and we landed at Leyte, Tacloban, Ormoc, Luzon,

Corregidor, and Wadke Island off New Guinea. Also we were on Bataan. Also we blew up Fort Drum, in Manila Bay, which is the fort we were supposed to blow up the night that Blue drank the compasses. We blew it up later and three guys died.

Before I gunned the engine I reached down real quick and loosened the knot and Blue fell in. His feet banged the gunwale. We were within couple hundred yards of two little islands and the water was maybe twenty feet deep. We'd tucked behind these little islands to be out of the sight line from the shore. I took off fast.

He might have made it. He was mostly sober by then and the water was warm. When we got back to base the lieutenant looked at the loose rope and didn't say anything and I didn't say anything. I told Mahon what happened but he didn't say anything either.

The regiment moved the next day and we never got back that way. I thought about Blue every day. After the war I met a boxer named Atlas Adams who had grown up with Blue. He said Blue's sister was the most beautiful girl he had ever seen. Blue was going to be a boxer too but he was a drunk. His sister married a guy who used to be a priest and they moved west. This was after the war. You should have seen this girl, said Adams. She was the most amazingly beautiful girl. You couldn't believe it when she opened her mouth and talked to you like she was a regular person. When she married the priest the mother cried and cried and the father just about went crazy. He used to stand in the street and just stare at their house, night after night, until finally they moved away.

HURTGEN

My dad was in the Hurtgen Forest during the war. The Hurtgen Forest is a dense woods on the border of Belgium and Germany. In the winter of 1944 the Americans fought the Germans there and some people say it was the worst killing field there ever was between two armies.

My dad never talked about the Hurtgen Forest at all until just a few weeks ago, when right after we said grace over the turkey at Thanksgiving dinner he got up and went out in the back yard and knelt down in the snow and cried. We thought he was going out in the kitchen to get salt or something but I heard the back door click and he was gone. I went out in the yard to see was he okay and there he was on his knees crying like a child.

That's a hell of a thing for a son to see.

After a while I got him to come back in. His knees were all wet and he went and changed his pants. No one said anything. After dinner people drifted off here and there but my dad started to talk about the Hurtgen Forest.

We were all just boys, that's the first thing to know, he said. Just boys. I was all of nineteen and there were none of us older than twenty. There were ten of us to begin with. That was the coldest darkest forest there ever was. The Germans were in there waiting for us. They knew we were coming. It was so cold you wouldn't believe it. Everything was wet. The trees were wet, our socks were wet, our rifles were wet. Our sergeant was twenty. He was a good guy. He got shot about ten seconds after we went in the woods. We all dove for cover. It was so dark you wouldn't believe it. You couldn't see a thing. One guy got up to run to a bigger tree and he got shot. He was carrying the radio, so another guy went to get the radio, which we were trained to do, and he got shot, and a guy went to help him and *he* got shot. So now there are six of us. We can't see a thing and we are scared shitless.

We had one guy seventeen years old who he lied to get in the army because he thought his girlfriend was pregnant, which it turned out she wasn't, but she told him she was anyway, but this guy, he was a Mormon, a little skinny guy, he lost it, and he and another guy, who was older, they couldn't stand it, and they jump up to run back out of the woods, a lot of guys did that in Hurtgen Forest, you don't see the army history books talking about *that*, but the second they stand up they get shot to pieces. There's brains all over. No one writes *that* down.

So now there are four of us, me and two brothers and another guy. The brothers start digging holes with their hands, figuring we are going to be here for a long time, and the older brother, they were from Boston, he reaches for his shovel just as a shell blows up in the trees right above us, and his arm gets blown off, and the kid brother, he screams and screams as his brother bleeds to death about five inches away.

Then the third guy, not the kid brother, he says well, we can't do a thing sitting *here*, boys, and he jumps up and runs right at the Germans firing his rifle, and he gets shot.

After a while I crawl over to the kid brother and get him to stop screaming. We figure we're done for. But the Germans never came after us, for some reason, and after a few hours some other guys came into the forest and get us out. We're all covered in blood so they take us to medical. When we get there a doctor says hey, it's Thanksgiving, Ike issued an order that every guy gets a hot turkey dinner today no matter what, can you believe that? Is today your lucky day or what?

About a year later my dad died and at his funeral there were a few guys who had been with him in the war. I looked at those guys, they were all standing together in the back of the church, and tried to figure out which one could be the guy who had been the kid brother in the Hurtgen Forest that day, but I couldn't tell. They were all sort of the same age, you know, the way men get to be after like age fifty.

Then at the house afterwards when people were sitting around drinking coffee and talking quietly and telling stories about my dad and hugging my mom and all a guy came up to me and said Can I talk to you a minute? and it turned out he was the guy, the kid brother who his brother bled to death in the woods.

The guy says quietly, Listen, your dad told me that he told you about Hurtgen, and I know this isn't the time or place to tell you what else happened that day, but I'd like to talk to you, whereas I don't have any kids and I am not going to live forever, and you young people should know some things, you know?

I say I know what he means because I have little kids now and already I have thought that there are some things I have to tell them to make sure they don't get lost, primarily for example my dad, whom they didn't really know except as Grampy, who could be remote as a mountain to them sometimes, to tell you the truth.

So a day later the guy comes over the house and we sit down over coffee and talk.

The first thing I should tell you is that your dad was a really good guy, he says. I mean you know that, but still. All of us respected him. We were all just kids but still. He was a really excellent guy.

Anyways, he says, the thing is, you know what happened that day, how ten of us went in and only two came out, and how my brother Billy died next to me, and how Joey Lemma ran right at the Germans shooting at them but they nailed him, but the part your dad didn't tell you was what happened then, between when he crawled over and when some guys came to get us out a long time later. That was a really long time.

All my dad said was it was a few hours.

Seven hours, says the guy. Seven hours. We went in about noon and it was dusk when some guys from the Second Battalion got us out. Seven hours. We were wet and cold and bloody and Billy was dead but his eyes were open, you know, like he was still looking after me. I think maybe I went nuts probably. But your dad crawled over and started talking. That's what I want to tell you, okay? Your dad told me stories. He just kept telling stories. All kinds of stories. Stories about kings and wizards and all, and stories about football and baseball, and stories about girls he knew, and stories guys had told him about girls they knew, and stories about animals and birds and stuff, and stories he read when he was a kid, and stories from different religions and all, and stories his dad had told him, all kinds of stories. He never stopped telling me stories, that's what I wanted to say. I don't have anything heroic and all to say. Just that. His voice telling stories, you know? Just that. But without those stories I don't get out of there alive, you know? It's important that you know that about your dad. Tell your kids that, okay?

Okay, I say, and he gets up to go, and we shake hands and all, and he goes, but a while later he sent me some photographs, one of which was him and my dad when they had just started being soldiers and were skinny as sticks. Wars are fought by kids most of which a good wind would blow them over and that's a fact.

WELCOME HOME DICK QUEEN!

The greatest party *ever* was the Welcome Home Dick Queen party, at the height of summer, a long time ago now, two weeks after Dick Queen, who was all of twenty-eight years old at the time, was released by the wild-eyed Iranians who had kidnapped him and sixty-five other Americans in November 1979. The Dick Queen party was everything you could ever want in a party—slightly too much to drink, melodramatic but harmless fistfights, people making out in cars and closets, a guy driving a car onto a porch, a cop arriving to break it up but staying and having a beer and eventually walking away laughing, and it didn't end until two days later. The only thing it was missing was a horse. Somehow a horse always makes a party better for reasons that are murky.

Anyway Dick Queen was released in July of 1980 after the Iranians noticed he was getting really sick. They were nuts but they weren't crazy, and they realized that a dead hostage would be bad television for the glorious revolution, so they let Dick go, but thirteen other hostages had been released before he was, so when he arrived back in the States it wasn't an especially big deal. This bothered my friend Jack, so he and his wife Susie decided to have a hell of a party for old Dick Queen and even invite him, all expenses paid, which they did, or at least they said they did.

The party started a lot earlier than it was supposed to because Susie, as she was painting a bedsheet with the words **WELCOME HOME DICK QUEEN!,** dipped into the party favors, and that sent Jack over also, and a few friends dropped by early to help set up, and they all got going too, so the party was roaring long before I got there after work on Friday. By sunset there were more than a hundred people throbbing in the little courtyard where they lived. It was a dense hot night in July and their apartment complex was right by a huge river so you could hear boats and owls all night long. By midnight there had already been a fistfight, so people were talking about that, and also two girls had slapped each other, a cold shocking awful sound, and then a guy no one knew showed up with a case of excellent wine. The cop showed up around two in the morning, and right there the party teetered on the edge, it could have shriveled and gagged, as so many parties do when the law frowns, but to everyone's surprise the cop totally got into it, because his cousin was in the foreign service, so when he ceremoniously accepted a beer from Jack a roar went up in the courtyard. That was the moment when the Dick Queen party started to be the greatest party ever. Another roar went up at dawn when the cop left, smiling and shaking hands as he made his way through the crowd to the courtyard gate. The bedsheet hung way up over the gate and the cop, a tall guy, reached up and touched it respectfully as he left, the way you would touch something holy.

When the sun came up people started making coffee but the party had its sea legs under it now and there was a good deal of whiskey in the coffee. A couple guys went to the bakery and bought everything and handed out rolls and pastries. People started drinking champagne with orange juice and the party revved up again, and new people kept arriving as others went home to sleep, and some people went swimming in the river to wake up and some went to sleep on the beach. By late afternoon the grill was going full blast and some guys with guitars and amps showed up and at sunset there was another fistfight, the kind where the combatants end up hugging and weeping, and then a rumor swept the courtyard: Dick Queen was coming!

Well, Dick Queen didn't show up, of course, I mean the poor guy was probably in a hospital somewhere, but the buzz was good for hours, and the party cruised smoothly into Sunday morning. The cop came back, off duty now, and he got drunk as a lord. Some of his cop friends came, and some new girls, and people came back who had gone home to sleep, but it was the most searing hot day imaginable, and finally the heat won and the party ended. The last thing I remember from the glorious Dick Queen party was a bedraggled Susie sweeping up broken glass on the porch and Jack snoring on the couch and Springsteen on the radio so loud you could see the music quivering in the air.

I kept an eye on Dick Queen after the party and he was a most interesting guy. He had endured the first three months of his imprisonment in a windowless basement room, and then his kidnappers let him go upstairs in the embassy, where he built a library for his fellow hostages and spent his days reading quietly until they let him go because they noticed he was getting dizzy all the time, which dizziness turned out to be multiple sclerosis. When he got home to the States he traveled around visiting the families of the other hostages until finally all the prisoners were released a year later. He then went back into the foreign service, which tells you something cool about the man, and he spent the next fourteen years in service even as his body failed and the divorce train hit him and eventually he died, only fifty years old.

Every time I saw his name go by I listened for what people said about Dick Queen and again and again the same words appeared: warmhearted, excited, patient, curious, never bitter, never the slightest rancor. *It happened to me but I won't let it get to me,* he said once, a line I never forgot. Also a lot of people noted that he was tall, so sometimes when I am having a dark day I imagine that Dick Queen *did* come to the Welcome Home Dick Queen party, a long time ago by a river late at night, and there was a tremendous roar, and he made his way through the party shaking hands shyly, and someone handed him a beer, and as he stood smiling under the bedsheet with his name on it in huge black letters he reached up and touched it for a moment like it was the most holy and amazing thing there ever was.

WAKING THE BISHOP

The late bishop was an enormous man and it took ten men to carry his coffin. Among the men were two nephews, big strapping fellows like their uncle, and a Buddhist monk the bishop had befriended in the latter years of his career.

The monk was a slight man and had to hold up his corner of the coffin with both hands. The nephews were up front and the monk was at the rear with the diocesan communications director, also a slight man. The other six men, representing various aspects of the bishop's life and ministry, were ranged along either side of the coffin, but as the communications director said darkly to the monk afterwards, It wasn't like those six fellas in the middle were doing a whole hell of a lot of work if you know what I mean.

The monk smiled but said nothing.

To get the bishop from the hearse up to the burial site at the top of the hill took major muscle, and none of the pallbearers spoke during the climb. When they reached the crest of the hill they set him down, their shoulders crackling with the strain, and stood silent for a moment waiting for the rest of the burial party to ascend. The monk noticed that the nephews' suit jackets were dark with sweat.

The big fella always did like the long view, said the communications director companionably.

It is a good place to rest, said the monk.

The rest of the burial party straggled up the hill and ranged themselves around the coffin and the auxiliary bishop led them in prayer and then spoke briefly of the bishop's endless capacity for kindness and humor, his personal warmth and grace, his admirable simplicity of style and consistent clarity of purpose, and his mindfulness at all times of Christ's insistence on love as the rudder by which we steer the flawed vessels of ourselves down the tumultuous and confusing river of life.

His metaphor license is expired, whispered the communications director.

Lowering the coffin into the hole took some doing, but two cemetery workers had come up to help, and they silently cleared away the ropes and planks once the bishop was properly in place. People tossed lilies of various colors onto the coffin—the late bishop had dearly loved lilies—and the auxiliary bishop tossed down a handful of dirt, saying, in his singsong way, *And God formed ye of the dust of the ground, and breathed into thy nostrils the breath of life, and so ye became a living soul, and now ye return unto the ground, for out of it wast thou taken, for dust thou art, and unto dust thou shalt return.*

Kind of a free translation of King James, eh? whispered the communications director as the two cemetery men stepped up with shovels and began to quietly cover the bishop. The monk noticed that the men leaned down into the hole with their loads of dirt and slid the soil gently onto the coffin so the clods and pebbles didn't rattle against the wood, and when they were done, and there was a mound of fresh redolent soil over the bishop, one of the men knelt and smoothed the mound with his hands.

Because the bishop had died on Holy Thursday he had not been formally waked, the events of Holy Week taking precedence, and the auxiliary bishop had decided that a big funeral at the cathedral on the Tuesday after Easter would cover the necessary public bases, which it had, and then some. The communications director had estimated two thousand people in the cathedral proper, five thousand or so lining the road from the cathedral to the cemetery, and untold thousands watching on live television in homes, schools, and offices. The television negotiations, as he told the monk, had been surprisingly smooth; even the secular media understood the bishop's unique stature in the city, and for the first time in the communication director's career he had been able to play one request for exclusive access to diocesan officials against another for the greater good of the diocesan coffers.

In the flurry of events there had also been no time to read the bishop's will, so the diocesan chancellor arranged for the interested parties and a few of the bishop's friends and colleagues to gather at the bishop's house after the burial. The house was on the campus of the university where the bishop has been president before his sudden and surprising elevation to the episcopacy; indeed the house had been built to his personal specifications by the university's carpentry crew, and thus featured a bathtub as big as a small pool, a greenhouse for the bishop's endless botanical adventures, and a vast back porch complete with an immense barbecue pit. The bishop had been very fond of grilling sausages and drinking beer, both of which activities, as he said, drew students like doughnuts draw cops. It was not unusual, remembered the communications director, for the bishop's back porch to be milling with a dozen or more students when he came by the house on diocesan matters of state.

The fact is, Jack, the bishop would say, I do more priestly work at the grill in an hour than I do in the chancery in a month. Maybe I should open a rib shack, eh? You remember Christ cooking fish over that little fire after He made his comeback, no one talks much about that part of the gospels, eh, but me personally I think the guy was a barbecue maniac. You remember the lines from your namesake evangelist, Jack: *Children, have ye any meat?*, my favorite line in the gospels, eh, and the poor hapless apostles mumble no, and Jesus then miraculously arranges for 153 fish to line up for the grill, and you remember the next line, Jack, *they saw a fire of coals there, and fish laid thereon, and bread, and Jesus saith unto them, Come and dine.* See? Barbecue as sacrament, Jack. It's right there in the good book. We have only to follow His glorious example and we will be fed. You want a beer?

Today, though, the bishop's back porch was empty and bereft, the deck chairs stored away for winter. It looks . . . forlorn, thought the communications director, and he thought of kindling a fire in the grill, for old times' sake, but the other guests were shucking their coats and moving briskly toward the kitchen and he followed them.

In the kitchen the university's cafeteria staff had laid a buffet, complete with various sausages, for they too had much liked the bishop, and the guests all loaded paper plates and drew coffee from a red urn nearly the size of a wine barrel. The auxiliary bishop was there, and the diocesan chancellor, and the university president, and two abbots and one abbess, and the lawyer the diocese carried on retainer, and the two large nephews, and a vice president or two, and a smattering of other priests and nuns. One nun was the tiniest woman the communications director had ever seen, hardly four feet high, and he realized that this must be Mother Thanh, superior of the Vietnamese nuns, of whom the bishop had often spoken with affection and respect, and to whom he had devoted much of the fading energy of his last years.

They're relentless women, Jack, he would say, and they don't take guff from anybody for all they are so tiny and smile so polite. Half of them survived seven hells and the other half worse. You mark my words, Jack, they'll do great things. Mother Thanh, now, she's intent on opening a hundred schools, and I bet she will do it, too. Woman has about eleven cents in hand and already two schools going great guns. Should make her bishop, that's what we should do, and then sit back with a beer and watch Rome burn, eh?

For a while the guests talked shop and quizzed the garrulous university president about the university's capital campaign and discussed zoning and demographics and parish registration rates and the status of the impending diocesan campaign against a statewide assisted suicide ballot measure, and then the diocesan chancellor told a story in her gravelly voice about the time the bishop had to ride a horse while blessing a new rodeo ring, which set them all to laughing and broke the ice, and then out poured the stories—about the bishop's pet parrot, a vile creature who hated everyone except the bishop, and about the way the bishop scooped up handfuls of acorns on his travels and carried them blithely through customs in his coat and tirelessly propagated them in his greenhouse, and how he held court at the university reunion every summer with a tankard of beer as big as his head, and how he once had a mule carry champagne and steaks on a camping trip, and how he often spent as much as ten hours a day listening to confessions, and how once when someone had thrown a stone through his window in protest over something or other he had had the stone engraved with the words *the stone thrown by the one who is without sin* and presented it to the chancellor in celebration of her many years of service, and how he never gave a sermon or a homily more than three minutes long and never delivered any talk of any kind whatsoever without a joke in it like a seed, and how he carried a salami in his car and had one in his desk *for emergencies, eh,* as he said, and how he cheerfully presented dignitaries with salamis which led to many hilarious photo opportunities, and how he had been the classmate of the pope at divinity college in Rome and the Holy Father chaffed him ever after that if the bishop had been more interested in academic matters and less interested in Roman *salumi* then maybe their roles would be reversed and the pope would be wearing a purple hat and the bishop the white robe, and this story made them all roar with laughter, for all of them had heard the bishop say cheerfully that if *he* was ever sentenced to the papacy God help us all the Church Eternal would immediately close up shop having proved itself madder than a wasp in a jam jar.

Well, I suppose we better get to the business at hand, said the auxiliary bishop, and they gathered up their plates and cups and put them in the sink and moved into the living room. The lawyer spread his papers out on the glass coffee table. The diocesan chancellor, with something of a proprietary air, sat down in the bishop's reading chair, and the university president, smiling, leaned back in the recliner and said something about beer and salami which made his vice presidents laugh.

The bishop's estate is somewhat complex, said the lawyer, given his vows of poverty, his membership in a religious order, and his long service to the diocese. There was a small family trust of which he was the sole beneficiary, his sisters having predeceased, and he assigned that to the diocese, specifying that it be used to foment vocations to religious orders. I have here a signed instrument making Mother Thanh the executor of those monies on behalf of the diocese.

Mother Thanh, who was standing near the television, bowed.

Additionally, continued the lawyer, the bishop over the years received many personal gifts from friends and admirers, all of which he was constrained by vow to present to his order, which years ago established a scholarship fund at the university in the bishop's name to receive such gifts. I am assuming that gifts made now in the bishop's name will go toward that fund, isn't that right, Father?

We certainly hope so, said the university president from the depths of the recliner, and everyone smiled.

As regards personal effects, continued the lawyer, they are disbursed in a detailed document I can read aloud if necessary.

No, no, Michael, said the auxiliary bishop. There wasn't much. The chancery will see to the distribution of his effects. I think we can be trusted.

What about the parrot? said one of the nephews suddenly.

Hmm, said the lawyer. I don't see anything here about the parrot.

Where actually is the parrot? said an abbot.

We have him, said Mother Thanh quietly.

I want the parrot, said the nephew.

I would suggest that perhaps we can work out custody and visitation schedules later, said the university president smoothly.

It belongs to us, said the nephew. I'm not saying I like the bird. I can't stand the thing. It's a mean animal and it bites. But it belongs to the family and it should be the family that decides where it goes. You all have taken everything else he had and at least we should get the parrot.

Exactly correct, said the other nephew.

These are *very* good points, said the auxiliary bishop, and the desires of the family are of course paramount at this time of bereavement and loss. Jack, will you arrange a meeting among the interested parties?

Of course, said the communications director.

Now as to the house, said the lawyer. It is of course university property, the bishop being resident by invitation, and the furnishings, with the exception I believe of the recliner, are also university property.

I bought the recliner for him, said the chancellor suddenly. He had the bad back, you know. It was a birthday present. A personal gift.

Does the diocese. . . ? said the lawyer.

I think perhaps it should stay with the house, don't you, Father? said the auxiliary bishop to the university president.

Absolutely, said the university president. It will remind us of the bishop.

The chancellor started to say something but then fell silent.

At this time then, said the lawyer, I will ask for everyone to convey keys to the house back to the university, and the communications director and auxiliary bishop detached their keys from their key rings and placed them on the table. The communications director was interested to see Mother Thanh produce a key and hand it to the lawyer. One of the vice presidents held up his key to show everyone the university's key.

That's four, said the lawyer. As I understand it there are five keys.

There was a long pause, and then the chancellor angrily opened her purse and took out a key and dropped it on the table with a clatter. The lawyer reached for it but she suddenly bent and snatched it up again. No one said anything for a moment and then the auxiliary bishop said, Dorothy . . .

Don't, she said. Don't lecture me. Not today.

Dorothy . . .

Don't, Ken. Don't give me advice. I can't bear this. I just can't. This is his house and his chair. This is *his house*. It's his *parrot,* for heaven's sake. And you all just sit here calmly. It's all so cold. How can you sit there and just *talk* about him like this? *How can you?*

Silence.

Not today, Ken, said the chancellor. Not today. No wise counsel in times of bereavement today. Take a day off, okay?

No one said anything for a long moment and then the chancellor leaned down silently and put the key in the center of the table with an audible click.

Well then, said the lawyer carefully, I think we are done here. Thank you all.

What about the parrot? said the first nephew.

Jack here will be in touch about the bird, said the auxiliary bishop, staring at the chancellor.

You know, said the communications director quietly, why don't we step into the kitchen with Mother Thanh for a moment and talk this over? I'm sure the bishop would much prefer that we settle this with humor and grace if possible, and where better for those virtues than this house? Mother, if you have a moment?

Mother Thanh moved without a word toward the kitchen and the university president hoisted himself out of the recliner, which returned to its former position with a sigh. The auxiliary bishop took the chancellor's elbow and asked her about a school dedication the next day and they were followed out the door by the rest of the party. The burly nephews moved toward the kitchen and the communications director heard Mother Thanh's quiet flinty voice embrace them.

Give me two minutes, folks, said the communications director in the direction of the kitchen, and he headed down the hallway toward the bathroom. He thought for an instant about hauling out the deck chairs and putting them in a circle around the grill like the old days but concluded that would look even more forlorn, so he continued down the hall. As he flipped the light switch in the bathroom, though, he suddenly heard the bishop's voice in his head, *Jack, with your permission I'll be stepping down the hall to see a man about the purchase of a horse*, which is what the bishop would say whenever he was in the same position, and hearing the bishop's grinning voice in his mind made the communications director suddenly immensely hilariously happy—happier, as he later told the monk, than he had been in a very very long time.

THE TRAIN

He'd walked to the station, and bought a paper, and found a corner seat on the train—about midway, so he could get out closest to the stairs when the train arrived in the city. Matters were auspicious—the weather fine, the news surprisingly positive about the machinations of his fellow creatures, the train car clean and uncrowded. He'd even gotten the very last paper in the kiosk.

He ran through the day idly in his mind as the stations flashed past—meetings, projects, lunch with his sister, a reception for John Mahoney upstairs. Mahoney was retiring, after forty years with the button company, and there would be drinks and speeches for an hour. He rather liked Mahoney, though he hardly knew him; Mahoney was a well-appointed man in a simple way, his jacket clean and pressed and his fedora in good order. Good shoes. Not much money in the man's pocket, he guessed, but a quiet dignity, despite his profession. Mahoney was a button-holer, a man who made button holes. To spend a whole career making holes! There was a joke there, or some great wisdom. He pulled out his notebook and made a note of the thought, for the day when he would sit down and write a book of such things. Maybe when he retired.

Between the stations—and there were dozens, as he caught the train at the far eastern end of the line—there were the familiar scenes of a morning on the train: the rear windows of three-flat houses, with an occasional glimpse of a woman within; the swelling hills of two cemeteries, with their marching headstones; the vast parking lot where the city's buses huddled yellowly for the night; a few open fields still. More properly vacant lots, he supposed. Fewer of those than there used to be, when he'd first started taking the train. Then it seemed that the train ran through the country, with a flash here and there of a citified thing, a gaggle of houses or a line of stores or a long low-slung factory with sad windows. Now it was the reverse—one long rattle of backstage urban life, with here and there a sudden snatch of something green. There was one last grove of trees, about midway through the trip—maples, he thought, from the broad flat star-shaped leaves, what little he could see of them as the train rocketed past. He made a point every morning of paying attention to the grove, out of some vague respect.

It happened right after the maples. He was in the middle of the paper, enjoying the prickle and bristle of the columnists, and reaching for his notebook to write down the thought that an opinion columnist needed villains for a really good column, when his chest roared with pain—a stabbing savage fire, a massive twisting of pain that doubled him over instantly.

He dropped the paper and immediately the kid next to him picked it up.

He was terrified. The pain was savage, awful, searing, the worst pain he'd ever felt, worse pain than he could have ever imagined. Something was wrong inside him, something had broken, something major.

He tried to sit up but the pain came again, ferocious and sneering and utterly dominant, and he doubled over again and closed his eyes and began to sweat.

He was as scared as he had ever been. His sweat soaked through his shirt and the thought flickered that he should remove his coat but the idea of standing to peel it off was ludicrous.

The pain receded a little and he managed to sit up again. The kid next to him and the two women across the car were all staring. Then the pain roared in again and he doubled over.

This went on for two more stops; each time the train lurched to a stop he desperately held onto his seat and tried to sit up for a moment but once the train picked up speed again he fell back with his head between his knees.

His back hurt too, he noticed from someplace deep in his mind—must be the sharp of bending. Just what I need now, a blown back.

After a while he noticed that the pain would crash and fade, crash and fade, a cycle, and he worked to rearrange himself in his seat to cushion against the worst stabbing. The pain slowly spread to his shoulders too and then out along each arm.

This must be a heart attack, he thought.

The kid next to him kept staring but the women across the car pointedly were looking away; he was a little embarrassed. They must think I'm drunk, or crazy.

Wonder if the kid wants my wallet.

Suddenly the kid opened his mouth, a thin slash in a thin face, and asked if he could help?

No, thanks. I'll be fine. Thanks.

He suddenly thought of the station in the city, and looked out the window to see where they were. Still ten stops to go! Then the station downtown, with all those people . . . what am I going to do?

By now he could sit normally when the fire ebbed, and he'd timed the cycles sufficiently to brace himself when he knew the awful part was coming.

Eight more stops.

He noticed, this time was real shame, that he had wet his pants, and when the pain receded he removed his hat—which was also soaked, he noted—and placed it carefully in his lap. A good hat, a man's hat, sturdy and friendly.

I'll call Ethel, he thought, if I can get to a phone. Where would she be now? Probably just walking back from getting the girls to school. But what could she do? Take the train in to rescue him? And even if she did that, managed to get herself into the train and to the city, then what? She couldn't carry him. And where would she take him? We can't afford the hospital.

I'll go to the office, he decided.

Six more stops.

Another jab of pain so fiery and mean that he began to weep without a sound.

He suddenly thought that he could ask the people in the car for help. They could call a policeman. He looked around: the kid, the two women, three men in suits, one guy in coveralls yawning, coming home from a night shift. Not many people compared to some days. Some days he was jammed against people so tightly that all you could do was make jokes. The price of living in the city, eh? We hardly know each other. I don't get this close to my wife. That sort of thing. When the doors opened at a stop you could feel the whole car sag out through the door, a sort of mass exhaling. It could get uncomfortable but all in all he liked the train and its people; the man who is tired of people is tired of life, said somebody. Samuel Johnson? He couldn't remember.

Four more stops. The pain had stopped at his elbows, he noted. It was clearly a heart attack—massive pain in the chest, burning and numbness along the shoulders and arms, sweating and nausea, although he also guessed the sweat was from pure fear—adrenaline, wasn't it, produced when the body faces sudden stress.

When the savage pain came he ground his teeth and closed his eyes and tried to go out of his body, counting slowly to twenty—twenty seconds at a time seemed to be the duration of the cycle.

I might die here on the morning train, he thought suddenly.

Two more stops.

I refuse to die on the train. My corpse on the platform and a crowd of people staring at my wet pants.

One more stop.

I'll get to the office and call from there. If I could lie flat and rest maybe this will go away. I'll ask Beatrice to call. She can call Ethel just to alert her and then call a doctor. Doctor Galvin maybe. But he's back at the end of the line. I don't know anyone in the city. Twenty-two years I've worked there and I don't know anyone, really. I know Mahoney. Button holes. A hole life, as Beatrice says. Nice woman. Glad she found a husband. Ancient Order of Hibernians. Good men. Irish Catholics. Reminds me of Maurice O'Sullivan.

Great book he wrote, *Twenty Years A-Growing*. Wrote it in the Irish, you know. Translated it himself. Gave me a copy. Lovely man. Met him at a Hibernians meeting. Died young. Shame.

The train stopped suddenly with a scream of brakes and he fell forward off his seat onto the floor, startling the kid, who leaped out of the way.

For a second he lay there staring at the flecked grain of the floor of the car, runneled so that water from boots and shoes could drain out. Then without a thought he leaped up and fell back into his seat. On the floor! Face down like a drunk! He sat stunned and so missed the count for a cycle and the pain hit him like a truck, doubling him over yet again. He felt ridiculous and broken and scared and angry all at once and again began to cry.

The people flooded out of the car, avoiding him.

A cop poked in looking for drunks and the sight of the cop was enough to make him stand up and walk briskly out into the dank loud busy station.

He looked desperately for a seat or a surface of any kind on which to sit and rest for a moment. Nothing. A horrible stab of pain sent his mind spinning. Hibernians. O'Sullivan had another book written, he mentioned one night after meeting. Not translated yet however. Died before translating. Ethel telling me of O'Sullivan dead. Met me at train station to tell me. Ethel weeping. Another Blasket man dead. Blasket Islands dead, all dead.

Another roar of pain inside him and he sat heavily on the stairs leading to the street.

I have to ask for help, he thought, again feeling as if his mind was in a country far from his body. I have to ask someone.

I won't do it, he thought angrily. They have things to do and so do I, and he staggered up again.

Holding tightly to the wooden rail, heedless for once of splinters, he hauled himself to the street level and out into the bright morning. The crisp light hit him in the eye just as another stab of pain in his chest did. Pain worse. Worsening. Worst. His mind sang grammar for a moment, good better best, and then fell all the way into Gaelic, a tongue he had not spoken for twenty years, a tongue he detested, the poor people's tongue, the very sound of it a rock in his mouth, dirt and poor people and mean weather and cows and dead children and everything he did always wrong. *Is baisteach ar fhuinneoig ina clagarnaigh, gan sanas air o thitim oiche* popped into his mind, the rain is a tattoo on the window, unslackening since the fall of night. That's a slab of a poem, he thought.

He shook his head and looked for the bus stop. Bench. Sit. He sat and clenched his hands and ground his teeth and waited for the bus.

I'll call Ethel now, he thought. No, later. Beatrice. His mind wandered. Poor boy, *an bhuchaill*, you need the hand of God on your brow, *go mbeanni Dia tu*, God keep you forever.

Here's the bus. Reaching into his pocket for change his right arm was so riven with pain that he blacked out for an instant and tripped on the top step of the bus and nearly fell into the lap of the bus driver, a burly man with a face the map of Cork. *Nil einne beo nach bhfluair oilean, is trua a chas ma theigh*, he said to the driver without thinking. The driver gaped at him and gestured at the coin box. He dropped in a coin and grabbed a pole and spun into a seat, his head reeling. Sweet Jesus, he thought. Help me. More poetry, that's Sean O Riordan, each of the living has found an island, and he who left it is lost.

By now the pain was a companion, a monkey on him, a companionable devil, he knew its ways and its story, and he fought it hard for the four stops uptown. Wary of the pain in his right arm he used his left to pull the bell-cord and was rewarded with a rage of pain worse than the other, and this stab too caused him a moment's blindness. *Le gra dhuit nil radhard im chionn*, I have no sight in my head, he said gaily aloud, and felt his way off the bus, his head whirling, the other passengers staring.

His sight cleared after a moment but now both arms hurt as badly as his chest. He drew himself up straight, went to adjust his hat, and found that he had lost it—it must be back on the train. A shame, a fine hat, he thought with a moment's lovely idle contemplation, and then another stab of pain set him shuffling toward his building.

As soon as he began to walk, though, his mind went reeling away into black shards and old songs and it was all he could do to maintain a semblance of dignity. He was aware of himself physically, as if on auto pilot or cruise control, and his body-sense of himself was gratified to see that he was moving correctly, walking along the pavement with a good clip, arms swinging slightly, smile on face. Cop on corner. Cooney, good cop, saved a child from burning building two years previous, good man, always courteous, said last night he'd be at Mahoney's retirement today.

Walk past Cooney and say hello normally, he told himself.

Mo ghra go daingean tu, he said, to his intense surprise, and Cooney's mouth fell open, just like in the movies. He kept right on walking past the gaping man, his body moving at a normal pace, as the splinters of his mind thought shrilly 'my love and my delight?!' You said that to a cop?!

He fell on the stairs, twice, one time all the way back down to the landing, but by now he couldn't feel anything, really, and he didn't even rest, there in a heap on the wooden floor. No runnels and no flecks, he noted distractedly. Back up the stairs, holding the railing with both hands. He'd wet his pants again, apparently, and he noticed that the right arm and side of his coat were very dirty, so dirty that he could hardly recognize his own piece of clothing. Ethel had given him this coat as an anniversary present, their tenth anniversary, she'd saved for it secretly, and when he opened the box late that night by the fire and lay eyes on the lovely camel coat she'd grinned that crooked open smile that made him shiver with pleasure. *D'ealaios om charaid leat I bhfad o bhaile leat*, he sang in his head, I had eyes for nothing else and love for none but you, and he fell again, this time heavily and permanently, a few steps from the office door.

It was Mahoney who found him a few minutes later. He had come downstairs to smoke a cigarette on the landing, the last morning cigarette he would ever have, he'd decided. A man has to do something with his retirement, make some plans and resolutions and changes. You can't just quit and then sit home. You have to look at retirement as a new start, a sort of emigration from one country to another, and the new country a bright one, rich with possibility.

CHINO'S STORY

Yeh, I shot the guy, everyone knows that, what with the play and the movie and all, and the thing is still in rotation at every earnest flyblown threadbare theater company in America, so no matter where I go, there I am, Mister Plot Device, shooting Tony so he can die in Maria's arms so everyone can weep and wallow in the Romeo and Juliet analogy as the music swells, but the fact is that while yes I *did* shoot Tony, who eminently de*served* to be shot for reasons I will explain later, no, he *didn't* die, I just winged him actually in the clavicle, it was like a *shaving* cut, and it was old Larry Kert, the original Tony in the Broadway production, who got the idea during rehearsal that he should *die* from being shot, and Jerome Robbins and Leonard Bernstein went all weepy about the idea, so that's how in the movie old Richard Beymer dies in Natalie Wood's arms, which is a total joke because old Richard Beymer would rather have been in George Chakiris' arms, you know what I'm saying?

But no, now everyone on earth has seen the movie, and everyone thinks old Chino killed Tony, poor Tony, cut down in the flower of his youth etc. but I am here to tell you that old Richard Beymer had a long and flowery rest of his career, you know what I'm saying, and the real Tony got busted for impersonating a pharmacist and robbing a deli, among other adventures, but old *Chino* never got a job in the theater, no, because who wanted crazy *Chino* in any of the parts that *Chino* actually was eminently qualified and *itching* to play, such as Estragon or Polonius or whatever, but no, every callback I got was for a nutcase, and me personally I feel there are enough nut cases in the world without me prowling the boards with a plastic pistol ranting and shooting daisies like old Richard Beymer who then get to cop a feel off the heroine as he dies in her arms etc. I mean, how come old Chino never got to explore any Natalie Wood topography, you know what I'm saying? But no, it's old Richard Beymer who gets to do graduate landscape study, which you have to laugh at the irony.

I remember Bernstein, who was about the size of a poodle, moaning with pleasure about Narrative Arc and Analogy and all when old Larry Kert shouted *hey, Lenny, I should die!* in rehearsal, but I knew immediately it was the end for me, I saw my future prance out of the theater like old Richard Beymer, not to mention my chance to get in a little technical advising action with Natalie Wood because everyone knew she was going to be Maria in the movie and I was going to gravely and in the most professional manner share the inside dope on street lingo and gang ritual and all with her which would have impressed her with my gravitas and all, and who knows where that would have went, because as far as I can tell real gentlemen were few and far between around Natalie Wood, not to mention at the time I was about the only guy in the room who didn't want to personally advise George Chakiris, you know what I'm saying?

Anyway I did summer stock for a while but there's only so many times you can do *Finian's Rainbow* and *The Fantasticks* and such without getting into *major* recreational drug use, and the end came for me one night during a *Carousel* touring the Canadian maritime provinces, I just couldn't bear it anymore, the cheerful relentless singing, you know, the songs bursting out of the narrative like boils, the only lower hell from there is *Oklahoma!*, you never want to be in a production that ends with an exclamation point! so I give up being Billy Bigelow! and go into business with some guys I met who do props! Mostly we do sets and all, specializing in fake fire escapes for gritty urban scenes, and fake ponds in which Ophelia drowns herself, and sets for Sartre and Beckett plays, which they're easy, just pretty much chairs and sand, you know, but we take a real professional pride in being able to find or make whatever is called for, so the other day when we get an order for a whole *West Side Story*, alpha to omega, total p-and-e, props and equipment, the whole gig from Officer Krupke's nightstick to Maria's shawl, you know, and I get to the end of the order sheet and find the very last item is "Gun For Chino to Kill Tony," all I can do is laugh, because we beat on, boats against the current, borne back ceaselessly into the past, as somebody says at the end of some stage adaptation of something or other, you know what I'm saying?

MALO

To get to him you had to go up through three checkpoints in the old house, each manned by two guards with guns, and then at the door of his room a guard put a gun to your head and stared into your eyes looking for a false spirit.

Even if the guard was your brother or son or father he held the gun to your temple for ten seconds while he examined your spirit. That was the rule.

If your eyes flickered that was the end of you.

At that time Malo was in bed night and day, there was some sleepiness on him, although he never seemed truly asleep, he could be spoken to, and he could speak thoughtfully in return, but never as crisply and authoritatively as before. Also he liked to have people in the bed with him, not for lurid purposes but just for warmth or company, a habit he said Gandhi had also adopted in the later years of his life.

So when I spoke to him at that time there would be people in the bed sleeping or listening, sometimes as many as four people. Also his room was filled with people sprawled on the low couches, talking in low voices. There were many telephones there but their ringing was muted and people spoke into them gently so the sound in Malo's room was murmur.

Malo had a fleshy face but was quite handsome still, and a broken front tooth that women always found attractive.

On the day the enemy came from the south I went to his room right away to tell him. By dawn the enemy was an hour from the house and pressing forward with great speed. This was what we had long anticipated and I ran to tell Malo.

Even that day the guard at his room stopped me and stared long in my eyes. He was the nephew of a man I knew but even so: ten seconds.

Malo did not move or open his eyes when I reported the enemy in the south but the people in the bed rose and left the room.

What we feared has come, I said.

I hear you.

What are we to do?

I don't know.

We must do something.

Must we?

We must.

I don't know, he said again.

I stood there listening to the murmuring of the muted telephones. Outside the room there were voices and in the courtyard below the window there was a commotion: shouts, trucks, running feet.

We have to fight, I said.

Someone always fights, he said.

We're responsible for the people.

The people will do what they do.

You should say something to them.

Should I?

From the window. Like the old days.

At this he opened his eyes and smiled and there was the famous tooth.

Like the old days, he said.

He emerged from the bed slowly and stood in the window. In the courtyard a woman saw him and cried out. He stepped out on the little balcony and raised both hands and the commotion below stilled.

Here I am, he said to the people craning to see him. Here I am. Soon there will be a wind among us. It comes in an hour. Such winds come and go. We come and go. Some will come and some will go. After this army another. It doesn't matter. Don't be afraid. Here I am. I will always be here. Here is what matters. We will always be together. We will always be here. Don't be afraid.

He stopped talking and dropped his arms and stood there smiling. For a moment no one spoke below; and then with a rush, as if there had been some subtle signal, everyone in the courtyard ran. Some people clutched their children under their arms like packages and others ran so blindly that they ran over children. Trucks slammed into gear and the dust ascended in thin golden columns like the trunks of immense translucent trees.

A CONFESSION

Bless me, Father, for I have sinned.

Tell me about it.

It has been, ah, it has been, well, it's been a long time, to tell you the truth.

A few years?

Less than twenty.

(dryly) Glad to have you back.

I used to be here every week, you know. I was a confession nut. Had nothing to confess then, though.

Speaking of confession, what would you like to confess?

I wouldn't like to confess anything, actually. But I think I should.

You do.

I do.

Why?

Being shriven of sins, that sort of thing. You know.

And your sins would be. . . ?

I covet my neighbor's wife. Well, we're not really neighbors, but he lives nearby. They live nearby. He and the wife. I'm a little nervous here.

That's a serious sin, you know. More than people think.

Yeh, I know. I feel badly about it.

How badly?

About half-bad. Half-badly, I mean. Is that a word, half-badly?

To be forgiven you must feel remorse.

Well, I do feel badly about him. Full-badly. He's a good guy.

And about her?

Well, about her I feel . . . covetous.

Have you acted on your desires?

Ah . . . yes.

More than once?

(Pause) You mean each *time* more than once?

(Pause) No.

(Pause) I think I answered your question.

(Pause.) Yeh.

So, *te absolve*, how about it?

It's not that easy, Jack. You have to be sincerely sorry and resolve not to sin again, to be absolved of sin. I'm not convinced that you are sincerely sorry.

Well, I'm sincerely sorry for *him*. He's got the depression thing too, you know. The black dog. And he's got a bad back. Jesus, a bad back is an awful thing. No matter what you do, there it is, like a knife in your spine.

Jack, for her you feel no sorrow? For luring this woman into a state of mortal sin, no feeling at all?

Hey, I didn't lure her. She had her high beams on, my friend.

So you're not at fault.

I don't think it's my fault, no. You know her. She'd dance with *you* if you could.

Okay. Let's get back to basics. Are you sorry for your sins?

(Pause) I'm sorry I hurt Mike.

That's all?

I'm sorry I got sucked into this, to tell you the truth. It stinks. We meet in motels and two seconds after I'm done I feel like a heel. But I keep going back.

Where do you meet?

At the Day-Glo.

Aw, c'mon. That's tacky. That's bad novel stuff.

Can't afford the Comfort Inn.

Jesus, Jack. On esthetic grounds alone you should break this off.
The Day-Glo. Jesus.

It's not that easy.

Why?

Well, for one thing, I paid in advance.

You're running a tab at an hourly motel?

You get a 20 percent break if you book in advance. Thirty if you
book more than a month.

How far in advance are you booked?

(Pause) Three months.

Three months. Jesus, Jack. That's embarrassing. The Day-Glo.

Uh—could we get back to the confession thing here? I got things
to do.

Shit.

Don't say shit in the confessional.

Okay. Listen, Jack—you have to stop. You know you want to. That's why you and I are here.

I know.

You only get the one life, Jack.

I know. But I'm tired. I don't care much anymore about right and wrong, you know? I don't mean to be rude or flippant, but I just don't. I just want to get by with a little jolt here and there.

(Pause.) It's a dark joy.

What?

Joyless. And cold. That's not what we're here for.

It's not hurting anybody. And I'm so tired of thinking about what I'm supposed to do. I just want to do whatever I want to do. I'm awful tired.

Me, too, Jack. Me too.

Bad days, huh? Even for priests?

Yeh, even for priests. Especially for priests. The nights are worse.

Yeah, but you know you're on the right side, you're God's boy.

Am I?

Aren't you?

I doubt it.

Hello? You're not sure of all this?

Nope.

So why are you telling me I'm sinning?

Because you're sinning.

How are there sins if there's no God?

Who said there's no God?

You did.

Fecking lie.

You just said you're not sure.

I'm not sure.

So what am I doing here then?

Trying to shuck your sins. Trying to shuck off the cold dark mean little things you do and are. That's why people come in here. That's why I am here. I don't have any magical powers. And this has nothing to do with whether there's a God or not. Who cares? This has to do with you knowing full well what's clean and true and what's the Day-Glo.

If you're not sure there's a God, why are you a priest?

I love being a priest. I love it because it's really hard and it doesn't make any sense. Therefore it's great. Like being married. Doing really hard things that don't make the slightest sense is what human beings are all about.

Jesus, Pete, I'm all confused here.

I believe in God, most days. It's harder at night. It's hardest when I think of all the pain and sadness. It's hardest when I think of kids, kids being beat up, kids getting worse things done to them, the worst things. Hard to believe there's a God sometimes when I see evil nose to nose, and I see evil nose to nose a lot, and it's evil with a fecking capital E, too. And it's lonely being a priest, and I got a heart murmur, and my balls ache, and here and there I have a second really big glass of whiskey and go to bed with my head swimming, and I eat too much, and I get real tired of the same people staring at me night after night in that bad swimming-pool light in the church basement in meeting after meeting of the fecking this or that committee on fecking this or that. I get tired of it. It gets to be a job. It is a job.

Quit.

Can't. Made a promise.

But if you hate it, why not bag it? You only get the one life. You just said that to me.

You're not with me, here, Jack. I made a promise. You make a promise, you stick with it. Not because you promise someone else but because if you don't keep your promises there's no real you. You're just another liar. There's plenty of liars but not too many real guys. And who knows anything about women, you know? Not me.

(Pause.) Okay.

Okay what?

Okay, I'm done with, you know, what I was doing.

Really?

Really.

Why?

Because I'm done.

Is that enough of a reason?

What are you, a chick? I'm done. Believe it.

Okay. I believe it.

Good.

Alright then.

(Pause.) Look, somehow you believing me is what I need to believe me, which I don't understand, but thanks.

You're welcome.

Let's get a beer.

You owe me.

Fecking lie. You owe me like eight beers.

I got two words for you: Day-Glo.

(Pause). Okay. Beer's on me.

Okay.

Okay. But then you owe me seven beers. You can't snake out on beers you owe a guy. A guy who snakes on what he owes another guy—that's low.

Good point.

Damn right.

Okay.

Okay.

Let's go.

Okay.

Well?

(They go.)

MULE

To drag the prisoner properly behind a horse you had to have a horse, and there were no horses in the village square, so Peter was sent to find a horse. The rest of the men waited with the prisoner, who sat quietly.

Peter walked briskly down the hill toward the river, thinking that there might be a cart-horse on the road, or a horse pulling a barge.

It was a crisp October day, one of those days when the edges of things are cut cleanly against the clean sky. The leaves in the trees were golden although here and there, in patches and groves of maples and oaks, there were searing burns of red.

After about a mile he saw a big brown horse pulling a barge. The horse was enormous—sixteen hands high maybe.

He stood on the bank and shouted at the boat and to his surprise a boy came out of the cabin.

What do you want? said the boy.

I need to take your horse, said Peter. Pull the boat over and I will explain.

No, said the boy.

This is a military emergency, said Peter.

No, said the boy.

I'll cut him loose and take him, then, said Peter.

I don't think so, said a voice behind him, and there were two men of the village who had heard the exchange.

Peter ran on. He heard the men shouting behind him. He ran for another mile before he found another horse. This was more of a pony but it would have to do. Two old men were walking with it. The pony carried a sack of seed or corn that sagged from side the side as the pony waddled along. It was old and fat but looked capable of dragging a prisoner.

I need to commandeer your pony, said Peter, running up.

What? said one of the old men.

I need it right now to execute a prisoner.

It's wrong to put a murder on an animal, said the other old man.

Peter wrenched the animal's harness away from the first old man but the second man shouted *I am a priest* and held up a crucifix that he'd fumblingly yanked from under his shirt. His shout brought a handful of villagers to their doors and Peter cursed and ran on, not wanting to be held up by the villagers.

He ran up a hill to scout out where there might be horses. A long golden field ran down the whole swell of the hill to the south and at the far edge there was a mule. Peter ran down through the field as fast as he could go. The mule, startled at his approach, galloped away. It was a good twenty minutes before Peter could catch it and by then he was furious. He mounted the mule and kicked it all the way back to the village square.

The prisoner was still sitting quietly in the ring of soldiers. For a moment they thought they would have to send Peter for rope too but another solider found a length of rope in a wine shop near the square.

They tied the prisoner behind the mule. It took a while—no one had actually done it before and they didn't know if you put the prisoner face-up or face-down, or lengthwise, or what. Finally they looped the rope around the middle of the mule and tied the prisoner's hands and feet together at the other end of the rope, so he was curled in a ball.

The prisoner said that this position hurt his back a great deal but they ignored him.

The mule stood fairly patiently through all this but bucked twice when too many men came near him. Peter went to stand at his head and calmed him some.

He must be a one-man mule, someone said.

Finally matters were all settled and the knots checked but then they stood around talking again, for none of them knew if they were supposed to send the mule and the prisoner flying through the square to flay the prisoner, or just walk back to camp with the mule dragging the prisoner slowly. They were all young men and while they knew that it was traditional that the prisoner be dragged behind a horse they weren't sure of the exact details of the thing.

Let's go get an old man who will know, someone said.

So Peter was sent again.

He went back to the golden hill where he'd found the mule and there just over the lip of the hill, in a little dingle, was a little chapel and there were the two old men, the priest and the old man whose pony Peter was going to take but didn't. When Peter ran up the priest pulled out his cross again and held it up and the old man held his pony's head protectively.

Go away, thief, said the old man.

Peter explained about the prisoner.

Well, said the priest, the tradition is that a prisoner be dragged behind a horse only if he has been sleeping with the wrong person, female or male. It's a religious tradition. What has this man done?

He's the enemy, explained Peter. We caught him by the river.

But what's he done? asked the priest.

He's with the enemy, and they've done terrible things to you.

They've done nothing to me, said the old man. You were going to steal my pony, though.

I am protecting you, said Peter. They'll kill you.

You're protecting me by stealing my pony? said the old man.

We've done nothing to them, said the priest.

They want your land, said Peter. That's why we are fighting them.

He wants our land? said the first old man.

His *people* want your land, said Peter. Listen—when we drag a man behind the mule, do we do that fast or slow?

Has he slept with a woman not his wife? said the priest.

I don't know, said Peter. Yes, yes, he has. So—fast or slow?

Is there a witness to his crime? said the priest.

No, there's no witness, but we know, said Peter.

Did his wife accuse him? said the priest.

Okay, fine, forget it, we'll drag him fast, said Peter, and ran back to the square.

Fast! he shouted to his fellows. Three times around the square as fast as he can go!

They had a devil of a time getting the mule to move very quickly, but then finally one of the soldiers lost his temper and fashioned a whip from a willow branch and he whipped the mule as hard as he could, and the mule clattered off around the square, the soldier chasing after it whipping it until its hindquarters were bloody. The prisoner screamed steadily the first time around the square but by the second time around he'd fallen silent and the only sounds were the soldier and the mule panting, and the swish of the whip, and the clatter of the mule's hooves on the stones.

When the mule had done three turns they stopped it and two soldiers had to take the soldier with the whip over in a corner to calm him down. The prisoner was a mess and they cut him loose. Two soldiers wanted to bury the prisoner but their sergeant said they didn't have time. He told them to drag the prisoner to the river. The mule stood there panting.

Peter said that he should take the mule back to its field but his sergeant said they didn't have time. They lined up and marched down to the river to meet the other two soldiers, who said that a boy on a barge had watched them dump the prisoner.

Should we kill the boy? they asked.

We don't have time, said the sergeant.

I feel bad about the mule, said Peter.

He'll find his way back, said the sergeant kindly. Animals are smart. Don't you worry. As soon as we are gone it will head right home. Not to worry. Good job finding the mule, Peter. Well done.

THE FOX

It had long been his dream to travel in remote alpine areas, a dream that became pressing emotionally after his wife died, but he loved their children dearly and did not wish to be separated from them for even a day while they were of an age that an attendant and attentive father was, in his eyes and theirs, more crucial than before. But when the boys enrolled together in college in the east, and their sister was ready for her senior year at a university in the west, the four of them decided that circumstances were such that he could fade from view for a year; the children could live with aunts or friends during the winter break, and should an emergency arise on either paternal or progenic side, a call to an appointed friend would serve as a flag for immediate contact. The children pointedly did not ask where he was going and he did not know himself. In late August he drove them to their campuses, sweet last road trips filled with music and laughter and tears and milkshakes, and then he drove up into the mountains to catch the last days of high summer—the redolent weeks when the days were hot but the nights brooded on winter.

He slept in motels, dusk to dawn, and was in the woods early, aiming always for high reaches, timberline or above, where he could be washed by the shocking light. In late October the first snow fell above timberline; by December snow was everywhere in the woods. He supposed he should go south, following the light, but something about the mountain had him by the bone now, and he stayed. By Christmas he had learned to snowshoe. In January he rented a cabin, and late that month he haltingly set a trap line, something he had never done and previously had abhorred. Over the next two months he learned to kill and skin marten, bobcat, and coyote, the pelts of which he sold to a purveyor in town. He did not hunt but he did learn to use a small pistol to dispatch animals struggling in his traps; once it was a young elk, which he shot and left in a snowy clearing for ravens and coyotes to find.

In early April he found a fox in his traps. It was very young, was caught only by a toe, and it did not struggle when he approached. Its coat was lustrous; not at all red, but a deep dark russet—burnt umber, as his wife would have said. He removed his gloves and readied the pistol. The fox stared. His hand shook. He fired and missed. The fox didn't flinch. He fired again and missed again, the shot echoing through the snowy firs. He braced his right hand with his left and fired again and missed again. The fox stared at him. He put his heavy gloves back on and put the pistol in his pocket and knelt by the trap. He caught the fox's needle jaws with his left hand and popped the trap with his right hand. Keeping his left hand on the snout, he gathered its legs with his right hand and stood up. It weighed nearly nothing, no more than his children had weighed as infants, six or seven pounds, perhaps. It did not struggle but continued to stare at him. He stared back, utterly absorbed by its astonishing eye, the quilt of its coat, the eyebrows as black and fine as the ink sketches his wife had so loved, the huge ears the size of a child's hand.

"For Every Thing that lives is Holy," he said to the fox. "That's Blake, you know. With the initial caps and all. Exuberance is beauty, that's Blake too. The fox condemns the trap, not himself, Blake said that too. He was a chatterbox, old Billy Blake. He liked foxes. He must have seen foxes all the time. He lived in England, as you know. Everyone likes foxes. My children loved foxes. I told them fox stories when they were little. They were just your size, the size of bread-loaves or cats or whatever. We'd make up stories about foxes in the dark. My wife said we should write them down but I never wrote them down. Who writes down the stories they tell their kids? You just tell stories because they're your kids and you want to talk them to sleep. You just wing it in the dark, story-wise, you know what I'm saying? You just wing it in the dark. Metaphor for everything. I forget those stories now, though. So they're lost. Everything gets lost in the end. That's the deep story, my young friend. Things fly apart. First rule of the universe. Entropy. But the second rule is that no *energy* is lost. This gives us the hope of resurrection. You know what I'm saying? I assume you know your physics. Energy and mass. I assume there are physics classrooms for foxes in the boles of trees. Specializations of discipline after the first year of studies. Some foxes to pursue graduate studies in human culture, some literature, Reynard, Aesop, that sort of thing. And you have played hooky. It is a school day, no? I believe it is Tuesday. I am not quite up on what day of the week it is. I have lost such details. And here I am discussing physics with a fox. A pup, a kit, a child. And I am frightening you, child. Certainly I am. Instead of soothing you to sleep. Your heart is hammering. The selfishness of an old man. A garrulous one too. I must ask your forgiveness as we part. It has been a pleasure making your acquaintance. Perhaps we will meet again. I do hope so. My very best wishes and regards to the family. I suggest that you make tracks right back to class and buckle down to your studies whatever they happen to be," and on the word *be* he bent his knees and tossed the fox as far away as he could, to be safe. It twisted in the air and landed silently in the snow and shot away so fast that for a second he was unsure it had ever actually been there until he noticed that his gloves were soaked with its nervous urine. All the way back to his cabin he grinned at the intense scent and tried to remember fox stories and by the time he arrived he had remembered the bony outlines of twelve, which he thought was pretty good, all things considered, and he took his snowshoes off before stepping inside to make notes but instead of entering the cabin he turned and got in his truck and drove to town and called the friend.

THE MAN WHO WANTED TO LIVE IN THE LIBRARY

He was sixty years old, slight, without the spectacles you would expect of the librarian. Amused, amusing. Gentle but intent. Married, generally happily, children grown. Fit no easy category. Employed by a large concern where he was generally admired. No particular obsessions or neuroses. Moderate drinker. Health good. Skier, bicyclist. Fiscal conservative, social moderate. Pension plan. A curiously small personal library, the result of what he called his annual urge to purge, a sort of bibliographic spring cleaning, conducted on the fourteenth of June every year, the day Jorge Luis Borges died. No known secrecies, manias, mistresses, ponzi schemes, medical worries, religious craziness, vendettas, enemies, or psycho-complexes. Small jaunty mustache, looked rather like David Niven. Scar on right shoulder from polio shot as child. Scars on hands from work in machine shop as teenager. Scar on left calf from misadventure with a parrot. Otherwise no distinguishing marks. Last seen in person Tuesday at five o'clock by security guard at corporate campus during shift change; they waved at each other with the half-wave men make to acknowledge acquaintance. Car found parked neatly in library lot. Personal effects in car undisturbed. All four windows open exactly one inch. Wallet, keys, cell phone nearly stacked on passenger seat, covered with baseball cap (Seattle Mariners).

Wife says that a stop at the library after work was normal for him; says on average he stopped there three times a week, and often he would stay in the library an hour or more, ostensibly researching various writing projects but really, she suspects, just poking around, her words. Says he swam to the library on rainy days like a trout to a fly. Says he could be found at the library pretty much any time you didn't know where he was. Says he more than once asked her out on dates to the library. Says he made a point on their trips to other cities to pop into the library for research porpoises, the same damn joke every time, her words. Says their children used to complain that when dad took them to Saturday morning reading hour he was reluctant to leave after the scheduled hour and they had to fake tantrums to get him out. Says he knew not only each librarian by name but every janitor, groundskeeper, board member, and regular patron. Says he also appeared to know every storage closet, obscure corner, dim archival room, and square foot of wasted attic space in the library, and had pored over the original plans and designs, even unto the tenth set of blueprints, one page of which he had framed and hanging in the wine cellar. Says he once mentioned that he was second on the all-time list of patrons requesting books from other branch libraries in the county system and had ambitions to be first. Says she said to him at that juncture what kind of nutjob would set out to win the all-time book borrowing title and what sort of twisted soul would even contemplate such a ludicrous proposition to which he had no ready reply. Says he was not what you would think a man so absorbed in libraries would be vis-à-vis new technologies for libraries and indeed was riveted by ways they could elevate the library experience, his words. Says he dreamed and sketched all sorts of ways that you could eventually consume and digest books in all sorts of new electric ways having to do with holograms and energy transfer and digital resurrection, his words. Says he would go on and on babbling about seventh dimensions and librarial interstices and as yet undiscovered livable realities of story-centered structures in which so many stories were housed and shared that eventually the space was soaked and slathered by stories in ways perhaps inhabitable by readers who are in the end themselves composed of stories. Says despite being a library nut he was actually a sweet man and a good father and a good husband, all things considered, every marriage having its tide charts, her words. Says the only unusual thing she can remember in recent months was his repeated desire to live *in* the library, a desire always accompanied with a laugh as if it was a joke which it was clearly not, this was a minor sore point between them, she thought they lived sweet jesus close enough, her words, to the library, five minutes by car and fifteen on foot, she thought he was angling to live nearer the library by proposing something clearly two steps beyond the pale so he could negotiate what he wanted, a ploy at which he was a past sweet jesus master, her words.

Says the husband often mentioned how his buddy Jorge Luis Borges, her words, envisioned the universe as a great library composed of an infinite number of rooms, at the very center of which there is a vast circular book with a continuous spine, which book is God, who contains all the books ever made or to be made, God being the compendium of all other books, and many wandered in search of Him, his words. Says whenever he started burbling on incessantly about God being the Book of Books she would cheerfully remind him of bibliomaniacs like the late Tony Cima, of San Diego, California, who was buried under his thousands of books when an earthquake hit, or Stephen Blumberg, of Ottumwa, Iowa, who stole thousands of books from hundreds of libraries and museums and is in jail until hell freezes over, or Ralph Coffman, formerly of Boston, Massachusetts, who stole more than a million dollars' worth of books from the library *he was the director of,* you wonder if he's in the same cell as your boy Stephen Blumberg, the two of them forced to read nothing but Archie comics until the day when hell etcetera, her words.

Says her husband was most definitely not a bibliomaniac, although he often quoted his buddy Cicero that a room without books is as a body without soul, but that the husband preferred specific targeted collections, such as for example that of Melancthon, who possessed only the works of writers whose surnames began with P, or a friend of said husband who collected only the works of

Stewart Holbrook, who wrote a startling number of excellent and idiosyncratic books about loggers, drinkers, sailors, editors, printers, radicals, bums, lumber barons, builders of Utopias, criminals, sea captains, fishermen, reporters, barkeeps, madams and such, the list of subjects itself a poem, his words.

Says the husband would often awake from nap murmuring the words *Library of Congress*, and when she quizzed him on same he would sweet jesus rattle on incessantly about its eighty million books, maps, prints, photographs, and pamphlets, and how it grows by ten items per minute, as if she cared a fiddler's fart, her words. Says the husband also liked to quote Leigh Hunt on the pleasures of being walled round by books, and how they were at their best imaginative voyages, and how enjoyment of books expanded a man's circle of friends precipitously in ways remarkable, his words. Says husband, when in his cups, would drone on and on about the Bronte children, Charlotte, Branwell, Emily, and Anne, and how they wrote a whole tiny library of tiny books chronicling tiny fantasy kingdoms, and how the Holy Roman Catholic Church, God bless its ambition, tried assiduously for fifteen centuries to ban books, including sweet jesus Edward Gibbon, and how bookmobiles are the greatest idea since sliced bread, and how it's revelatory and suggestive, his words, that so many men of genius were printers or engravers of books, for example Franklin and Blake, and how we should all get down on our blessed knees like old horses twice a day and thank the Coherent Mercy for such glories as Giambattista Bodoni, who invented more than three hundred typefaces, and how it was also revelatory and suggestive that the first books Vladimir Nabokov read as a child in the family's country dacha were Albertus Seba's *Locupletissimi Rerum Naturalium Thesauri Accurata Descriptio* and the Grand Duke Nikolai Mikhailovich's *Memoires on Asiatic Lepidoptera*, and how the first book printed in American in America was a book of psalms, and how Evelyn Waugh was right that one definition of hell would be to be doomed to read nothing but Dickens the rest of your life, you would be sweet jesus a gibbering puddle posthaste, his words.

Says husband was fond also of moaning about the fact that some twenty million Americans cannot read at all and more than half of the population of the nation does not manage to read a single book in the course of a year, not even sweet Charlie jesus Dickens, his words, and that at the drop of a hat or not even that much ostensible invitation he would launch into a joyous paean to library stacks and shelves, and how trailing your fingers along the spines of books is like trolling for wonder, and how opening sentences are like bait, and how borrowing books from a library is such a sweet and generous communal act that perhaps it and collective public schooling and wise policing are the tendrils that hold society together, and how Pascal was right when he said that all men's miseries derive from not being able to sit in a quiet room alone, which is why, he, the husband, more than occasionally, her words, expressed the desire to be cremated and scattered among the stacks, and also more than occasionally, her words, said, ostensibly in a teasing manner although sweet jesus I realize now he was not teasing at all, her words, that he would at some point take up residence, either corporally or spiritually, in the library itself, and so read the next chapter of the Book of Books, his words. Says this is what she now suspects he, the husband, has in some way shape or form accomplished, and that we, the investigative team, are wasting our sweet jesus time, her words, seeking a solution to his disappearance, because, it sure sweet jesus looks like he checked in permanently to the very entity where so very often he checked out. Says where's his precious library card? Says she bets sweet jesus that his precious library card is with him, wherever he is, which someday she would also like to be, damn his evil bedroom eyes. Says if we are going by the library anytime soon can we check out the works of Borges for her? Says we should give his Mariners cap to whichever child will be thrilled to wear it. Says never mind about going to the library, she will go to the library her sweet jesus self right *now* and read his buddy Jorge sweet Luis jesus Borges, her words.

RAMON MARTINEZ TELLS WHAT HAPPENED THAT DAY

My name is Ramon. I am fifteen. One thing people don't know about me is I saved one of the airplanes on September the eleven from hitting one of the towers. South tower. No one knows this because I used my power to make everyone forget. There will be people say I say it now to get credit for this paper due in school but that is not the reason the reason is people should know what I can do so they don't mess with me. People did mess with me before and that is how I develop my power. It is a strong power as you will hear.

What happened was I was walking to school when a plane flew right above me and I knew immediately it was flying wrong. I am sensitive. I laser my ears on it and hear the screaming of passengers inside and the cursing of the bad pilots. Two pilots they cursing at each other fierce. I hear what they are saying, I understand all languages with my power, they are cursing each other about who gets to be the one who drives the plane into the tower and so be the hero and go to heaven. No time to lose! I drop my backpack and zoom right up and catch the plane. Have to use both hands. It is traveling I estimate one thousand miles per hour. Pilots looking out the window see me catch the plane and are shocked. Eight year old boy catching the plane! They start cursing worse than before but I have heard every kind of cursing, no cursing or hitting can hurt me, I have a secret shield, curses and punches just bounce off me, my mother's boyfriend he learned that lesson finally, no matter what he tried he could not hurt me, you should have seen his face! He cursed and cursed until I atomized him with my mind and made him vanish. That was the first time I had done that and I was scared but then I realized it was a gift.

The airplane was still moving slowly, you know, even *I* cannot stop a whole plane just like that, and it bangs me against a building, I think it is a hotel or a television building, but no hitting can hurt me anymore, I use my mind to send the pain far away like a letter in air mail. Then I turn the plane around and get ready to throw it where it was supposed to go, which was Chicago I can tell from the brains of the passengers, but before I do that I feel for the real pilot with my mind, but he is knocked out, but I wake him up with my mind, and I take the two bad pilots out of the plane by atomizing them through the window, and then I make everyone on the plane forget what happened and the real pilot thinks he had like a electric stroke or something for a second but recovered, and then I shove the plane toward Chicago, so everything goes back to normal. Then I take the two bad pilots who are hanging in the air cursing and vision them to a jail in Tanzania, which is a country we were just studying in school so the name is right there in my mind, and I atomize them to the jail. Then I quick land back in the street and get to school where I hear about the other four planes.

I was sad to hear about the other planes but there was nothing I could do, I was busy with the fifth plane, I think it was United but I am not sure. I was only eight years old at the time and just learning the power. That was the year I figured out how to make a cursing and hitting shield and how to make things happen by thinking about them. My mom cried about her boyfriend for a while but I figured it was better to let her think he just walked out than to confess that I atomized him. And sometimes I think about the two bad pilots they are probably still in the jail cursing at each other. Sometimes I lay in bed laughing thinking about the jail boss thinking he had like ten people in jail and suddenly he has twelve and no one knows who the new guys are or how they get there but no one knows how they get where they are anyways so you just do the best you can.

THE GREYHOUND BUS
IS YOUR MOTHER & FATHER

My friend Denny was born in 1954 on a Greyhound Scenicruiser bus, so he was, as he liked to say, born mobile & destined to be restless, which was true, as he never paid rent or mortgage, never had a mailing address, & was, as he liked to say, a verbacious man, transitory & travelacious, a man whom, after passing from this existence to whatever is next, would certainly still be a relentless voyager among the endless & impatient stars. This was how he talked, all metaphysics & ampersands, & he made a little swirl in the air with his fingers when indicating an ampersand, which is not the same as the thing people do when they make quotation marks in the air, which *that* drove him insane, to the point where he was always talking about carrying a ruler & waiting for people to make quotation marks in the air & then cracking them over the knuckles with the ruler while explaining that he was a teacher & his actions were required as condition of the renewal of his licensure by the state.

I dissuaded him of this, but he kept dreaming of it, because, as he said, people just totally glaze over when you use words like *licensure,* which is one of those words, like *embezzlement* & *hermeneutics* & *amortization*, that are instant soporifics, they squat in the air like toads, no one really has the slightest idea what they mean, like the word *hermeneutics*, he would say, you could look it up twenty times a day & it just doesn't stick in the old brain pan, you know? *The theory of the interpretation & understanding of a text on the basis of the text itself,* what in heaven's name does that mean? When a word like *hermeneutics* goes by in a conversation, he would say, the poor overwrought thing laboring through the air like a zeppelin, there's a respectful pause as everyone watches it groan past, & then the conversation gets back to beer & tires or whatever.

Such moments of pause & puzzlement, he would say, are the countries in which we are most truly ourselves, because then we are admittedly & openly uncertain, we shuck the usual confident mask, we achieve a brief & temporary selflessness in which paradoxically we approach honesty as nakedly as planets & comets behold the yearning & awesome sun. We are verbs, he would say, we are migratory, we are neither nor, we are Heisenberg's principle, we are immeasurable, we contain multitudes, we are the very incarnation of uncertainty, we are Max Planck's *in*constancy, you know what I mean?

≈

Some facts about Denny: He was physically slight but intense & weirdly strong, that kind of mad wiry strong that little skinny guys are sometimes, you know? Thin hair, sort of reddish. Quick wit, widely read, but not erudite-arrogant, not the kind of person anxious to show off how he knows more than you. A *very* good listener, which I think was maybe the key to his character. Decent athlete in solo sports, swimming & running & such. Terrible at every team sport. Complicated romantic life. Countless friends, male & female, old & young, human & animal, all of whom he kept until the end; he had an endless capacity for new friends. In business, an entrepreneur. He started all sorts of businesses & every one did shockingly well. They were all a certain *kind* of business, if you look at them as a pattern—subtle, almost obscure, enterprises: rubber bands for vegetables, cardboard inner rolls for toilet paper, bus shelters, nail clippers for mice & hamsters & ferrets & such, shoelaces in all shapes & sizes & colors & even flavors, the tiny screws & screwdrivers with which people repair their eyeglasses, newspaper kiosks, ice scrapers for cars, wire cages for new tomato plants, combs & brushes for left-handed people, a tool for scraping off bumper stickers, beanpoles for climbing beans, socks, dental floss in a hundred flavors, teapots, scissors in a hundred colors, ear-hair trimmers, measuring cups, coffee filters, things like that. The necessary ephemera, as he said.

His companies, in toto, made him theoretically wealthy, if ever the assets had been allowed to accumulate; but his habit was to keep the money flowing from one company to the next, so as soon as one company employed ten people & went over a million in gross sales he sold it to the employees & poured the proceeds into the next company making twist-ties, or soap-on-a-rope that smelled like roast chicken, or whatever.

I pointed out to him, as his financial advisor, that accumulating assets & culling interest would provide as much or more resource for entrepreneurial or charitable activity, but what appealed to him was the flow, the fact that the money, once created, did not, as he said, huddle & hide, snooze & brood, but *move*; which was the key for him, eternal motion & transition.

~❧~

After his death I made some discreet inquiries & it was indeed the case that he had been found in 1954 aboard a Greyhound bus originating in New Mexico & terminating in Oregon. A report filed by the driver stated that he had discovered an infant, male, age unknown, wrapped in a man's large cotton shirt (blue), on seat 25 upon the bus's arrival in Portland. *Child was not crying*, said the driver to the police stenographer. No list of the passengers was recorded & the driver could recall no women of child-bearing age on the trip. The baby was sent initially to Emanuel Hospital for examination & then remanded to the state's department of human services for assignment to foster care. According to the initial report filed in human services Denny was *approx. two days of age* on registration with the state, *parents unknown*. He had been given the name Dennis by a nurse whose beloved uncle of that name was recently deceased. For ease of registration & recording he was assigned a surname chosen at random by a computer: oddly, Dennis. One of his many projects afoot at the time of his death was a court petition for an official middle name, also Dennis; I had dissuaded him from his other candidate, an ampersand, although one of the last things he said to me was how Dennis & Dennis would be a *totally* cool name, he'd be like a one-man law firm, what was he *thinking* when he listened to me, how very often *my* sage advice had ended up leading to hilarious & *egreg*ious error on his part, what in fact did a meticulous analysis of our personal & professional relationship reveal but a vast *cav*alcade & parade of headlong errors too unbe*liev*ably long to list, perhaps what we *real*ly should do is establish a corporation called Muddle & Mistake Un*lim*ited, & etc. in this vein. This was also how he talked, a kind of running grinning commentary, as if life was a game & he was an announcer with an irrepressible sense of the ridiculous.

✑

From ages one to three he was in foster care with a family of five in Coos Bay, Oregon (on the coast). From ages six through sixteen he was in foster care with a family in Sheridan, Oregon (in the Coast Range mountains). At age sixteen he was admitted to Reed College in Portland, early admission, full academic scholarship. Colorful but undistinguished undergraduate career. *He was a remarkable student but essentially undisciplined,* his advisor wrote me. *Gregarious, popular, creative. A student who may be said to have enjoyed every moment of his college career but never found a particular focus for his creative energies. His subsequent business career was something of a pleasant shock to those who knew him here. We were startled & proud (you see he made us all use the ampersand too). You may have heard the story that after he died some students rearranged the letters at the front gate to read RE&ED as a tribute & there was a great hullabaloo when the administration repaired the sign; I cannot help but think that the outcry among the students would have amused Mr. Dennis.)*

☙

As his financial advisor at the time of his decease I found myself pressed into service as his executor, his business matters being complicated, & among the details I discovered were these: he had in total established twenty-seven businesses in twenty years; he had established two full scholarships at Reed for students from Coos Bay & Sheridan, respectively; he had paid for the refurbishment of the entire school bus fleets of the school districts in those towns; he had made a large gift to the Oregon Garden in Silverton for the planting of a rose garden in the shape of an ampersand one hundred feet tall; he had established trusts for the college educations of all children in both his foster families for the next fifty years, any monies remaining at that point to be contributed unrestricted to Reed College for use in upkeep of the college gardens; & he had, in 2004, a month before his death, quietly purchased the Greyhound bus company for fifty million dollars.

☙

The Greyhound bus company, now formally known as Greyhound Lines, Inc., began life in 1914 as the Mesaba Transportation Company, in Hibbing, Minnesota. It was invented by a Swedish immigrant named Carl Wickman, who carried iron-ore miners in a bus from Hibbing to nearby Alice, charging fifteen cents a ride. In 1915 Wickman joined forces with a neighbor who also owned a bus, Ralph Bogan. That year they made a profit of eight thousand dollars. Three years later they owned eighteen buses & made forty thousand dollars. Three years later they commissioned new buses, so sleek & gray they were nicknamed greyhounds. Three years later they expanded into Wisconsin. Five years later they were the Greyhound Corporation, worth many millions of dollars, with headquarters in Chicago. By the 1930s the company & its signature buses were ubiquitous & had even, in the final sign of cultural acceptance in America, appeared in the movies—a Greyhound bus plays a key part in the 1934 Clark Gable movie *It Happened One Night*.

The subsequent story of the company is riveting—strikes, troop transport during the wars, a chain of Greyhound restaurants (called Post Houses), expansion into Canada & Mexico, more strikes, bankruptcy, resurrection, mergers, a series of female greyhounds serving as corporate ambassadors at public relations events, the Freedom Riders of 1961 riding on Greyhound buses, blues musician B.B. King writing a song about Greyhound buses, but one odd detail jumped out at me from everything I read: Carl Wickman, the founder, who had retired in 1946, died in 1954, as the company introduced the Scenicruiser, the bus on which Denny was born.

∾⌒

Denny's offer for the company, I discovered in papers filed with the Securities & Exchange Commission, was for four times cash flow (six million dollars annually) plus the value of cash on hand at the time of sale (twenty-six million dollars), an offer that was accepted by the board of trustees with, one might say, alacrity. The chief executive officer at the time has since told me that while the board certainly would have accepted such a handsome offer for the company under any circumstances, they were, to a man & woman, impressed with Denny's calm honesty; he, the executive, remembered, for example, that Denny had said, forthrightly, that the company was essentially a losing proposition as constituted, but that there were any number of other factors to be considered in a transaction of this nature, & that one thing he, Denny, had learned in the conduct of his personal & professional affairs was to be alert & appreciative to all aspects & intricacies of exchanges & transactions, such being the cheerful & poetic coin of human commerce & discourse. *You could almost see the ampersands in the air*, said the executive, smiling. He also told me that Denny had told him that the single greatest sources of his wealth was sippy-cups for small children, in which he had cornered the market. The executive also told me that after Denny's death the board has authorized the christening of a bus in Denny's name—not a Scenicruiser, as those are no longer in circulation, but a G4500, the newest model, renowned for its quiet ride. The *Dennis Dennis*, said the executive, generally operated in Oregon, ranging as far afield as British Columbia & New Mexico. On it was affixed a small bronze plaque with a cryptic remark of Denny's, a sort of koan I too had heard him say occasionally: *The Greyhound bus is your mother & father.*

❧

Inasmuch as Denny at his death had left behind no papers, records, & notes of any kind as to his plans if any for restructuring the corporation, I instructed the board to have the company operate as was, pending further instructions, with all extensive financial decisions to be cleared through me as executor. I believe what Denny would have wanted is for someone with energy & creativity to operate the company in such a manner as to honor the legacy & character of a corporation that is in a real sense an American institution, while also being alert & appreciative to other aspects of transportation which may not reveal themselves easily to the eye jaded by long contact with business & commerce as usually promulgated & pursued in these tumultuous times.

I sought advice from Denny's many friends, an effort that as you can well imagine was a vast enterprise, & finally settled on a board of twelve men & women ranging in age from eight to seventy, with a rotating chairmanship period of a year (age being no bar to the chair). In the first year of trusteeship the board made a number of changes & enacted a number of programs & projects which drew what I would characterize as sometimes hysterical attention in the media. Among these programs, as the reader may recall, were the design & construction of buses sculpted in the shape of huge greyhounds; the advent of buses equipped with double beds & reading lights; the advent of buses equipped with thematic libraries; the experiment with buses that never stopped moving but accepted & disembarked passengers from small trucks nicknamed pilot fish; the design & construction of buses built entirely of transparent plastic; the experiment with obsolete buses being converted to mobile homes & trailers; the experiments with fuel made variously of corn, glossy magazines, milk cartons, kudzu, blackberry vines, ivy, cassette tape, & pulped paperbacks; the experiment with buses designed horizontally rather than vertically; the advent of bright orange racing buses; the construction of a bus composed of woven cedar branches; the brief incendiary experiment with buses running on rocket fuel; the advent of competitive bus racing initially in North Carolina & then throughout the south, which has turned out to be a remarkable cultural phenomenon; the boom in buses built in the shape of guitars & saxophones, for touring musicians, & footballs & baseball bats, for athletic teams; the advent of personal mini-buses (GreyPups); the buses shaped like Carl Wickman & Ralph Bogan with headlights where the eyes would be, which gave rise to the whole current fad for cars with faces; the rise of, & hullabaloo over, what is now called bus-culture, with its own lingo & music & fashion; the expansion of the company onto nearly every continent; the construction of athletic fields & stadia in the shape of buses; the reconfiguration of some routes to resemble ampersands; the renaissance of Hibbing & Alice as tourist destinations complete with theme parks & reenactments; & much else.

I will leave for other writers an account of the rise of bus culture, the new industries it sparked, & the political changes thus occasioned around the world; suffice it to say that Denny would have been delighted to consider that his entrepreneurial itch led ultimately to peace & employment in places formerly famous only for violence & despair. And too I leave for scholars a careful analysis of the Greyhound bus in terms of zeitgeist. Why so many areas of the world would suddenly seize upon the bus as icon, & use its image & utility to foment a remarkable surge in creativity in so very many areas of endeavor, I cannot explain; such consideration is beyond my analytical powers & my purview here.

❧

I should address the matter of Denny's death. He had just turned fifty, & was in fact on a bus (Greyhound) returning from a meeting with the board in Dallas, Texas, when he suffered what appears to have been a stroke or aneurysm of some kind. Response on the scene was immediate; by chance there were not one but two doctors on the bus, & the driver, a man named Hugo Sanchez, had in his previous career been a nurse specializing in emergency care. Despite immediate attention, however, Denny was beyond resuscitation, & he was pronounced dead just over the Idaho border with Utah. An autopsy performed at Emanuel when his body was returned to Portland could find no proximate cause of death; while his heart was found to be slightly enlarged, there was no evidence of failure. The formal conclusion was that he had suffered a silent stroke of sufficient trauma to cause his death; the informal conclusion, reached by his friends, is that Denny had moved along swiftly & without hullabaloo toward the endless & impatient stars.

The passengers nearest his seat, when questioned by the police, reported only that they remembered a cheerful & friendly man who made a point to greet each of them before retiring to the back of the bus to sleep. A woman named Adele Cohen, seated across the aisle, remembered seeing Denny arrange his jacket as a pillow, before she herself fell asleep somewhere in Oklahoma.

❧

It has often seemed to me that Denny slipped away from this sphere of existence in much the unadorned way in which he entered it; & this suits the theme & tenor of his life, which was, in so many senses, devoted to the idea that there are no fixed things or ideas, all is flux & flow, & that we are here not so much to be beacons as to be boats from which each hails & heals the other. The disciplines that most appealed to him where those of quicksilver nature, the ebb & flow of business, the growth & decline &

rebirth of plant life, the conundrum & delight of travel, in which the traveler can fairly be said to never actually *be* anywhere specific, but is, in a sense, always in motion. The temptation to march into metaphor here is very hard to resist, but the very notion of waxing metaphysical brings Denny's shout of laughter instantly to mind.

∾

Did you ever notice, he said to me once, that the word ampersand includes & concludes the very word that the ampersand itself represents? A case, he said, of a label for a thing being the thing itself. There should be a word for that phenomenon, don't you think? & don't you think really the way the ampersand should be written is *ampers&*?

I find myself these days using the ampersand in incredible doses, which interests me greatly. Was I so influenced by my friend that I have taken to adopting his mannerisms? Is that a sign of deep respect & affection, or a mysterious form of mourning & elegy, or something more convoluted & psychological? Is it perhaps a peculiar form of grief?

∾

This note is incomplete without discussion of Denny's romantic adventures, but that aspect of his life seems not only eminently private but certainly inexplicable, in any serious sense, to anyone, including Denny & the women whose company he so enjoyed. I think it is sufficient to note that he was a kind & attentive man in his conduct with women. I am told that no woman who loved him ever had cause to regret or disavow the time they spent together. That such times were relatively short is something to be noted rather than explored; who among us can explain his or her own romantic adventures & misadventures, & discern, among your series of lovers, any pattern other than the consistent yearning of your heart for understanding? So I can say fairly of Denny that he strove mightily to love & be loved, & if the testimony of those who loved him is to be believed, he was honest, entertaining, thoughtful, & kind. Is there a greater compliment to offer a man than to celebrate his kindness with women?

In this vein I also remember a recurring remark of Denny's, on the subject of marriage, that, in his view, the marriages he saw that appeared to be refreshing & stimulating for both parties, seemed to have, in general, a character of changeability about them; in fact they were, in his phrase, not one marriage at all but a long series of brief marriages between two people who changed constantly. A perceptive view, it seems to me.

∽∾

Similarly we might briefly contemplate Denny's relationship with children, a class of being he loved but did not find himself in a position to relate to in the orthodox biological sense. It would be more accurate to say that his relations with children were avuncular, & indeed there were many dozens of young people to whom his role may be said to have been brotherly, in the sense of an older brother who, while not resident with the nuclear family, still appears on a regular basis, savors meals, spends hours by the fire telling tales & playing chess, cuts the grass, cleans the gutters, changes the oil in the car, and buys beer without being asked to do so. Suffice it to say of his relations with children that which can fairly be said of his relations with women; no one who knew him at all well was not elevated by the experience.

∽∾

Eulogistic or memorial accounts of this sort also seem to require a note on the first meeting of subject & author, as if to give the reader a point of departure, but I don't see the need for it here. I knew Denny most of my life; we were instantly friends upon encountering each other; & were I to account our thousands of conversations, debates, arguments, discourses, jokes, tensions, misunderstandings, adventures, travels, & moments when we both stood mute witness to sorrow & to joy, this writing would stretch on to infinity. A pleasant thought, because the accounting of rich friendship is an accounting finally of what human beings are capable of at their best; but again I can hear Denny's burst of laughter at the very idea, so I desist.

※

It is interesting, again speaking as executor, that Denny left no written, visual, or aural recording of his life & thought at all. He was famously loath to be photographed, he wrote no letters, he declined to use electronic mail, he declined interview requests, & what we have of his writing is only his illegible signature on contracts, agreements, & forms. He kept no papers, harbored no library, committed no memoir. He was a great fan of the telephone & of what he called the incarnated conversation, or table talk; & it can fairly be said of Denny, as it was said of Robert Louis Stevenson at his death, that among the prime reasons to mourn such a loss is the sudden absence of a wonderful talker. I should say too, as his friend, that I do not know that there was ever such an excellent listener; very often, in conversations with him, you would realize suddenly with a start that you had been talking animatedly for a long time & he was listening with the fullest & most complimentary attention.

※

It would be a mistake to think a mere business transaction the greatest accomplishment of his life, & I perused the various obituaries with discomfort. His quiet acquisition of the bus company, his colorful commercial record, his vibrant personality—certainly these are inevitably important parts of his story, but I cannot suffer them to be *the* story; Denny was far more than a deft businessman, or a man entertainingly set on restoring the ampersand to modern life, & I write these notes to try to account some of his character & depth. He was that class of man who, once he has entered your life, never leaves it, for his humor & wit, generosity

& verve, vibrancy & curiosity, cheer & zest, become necessary fuel for your own existence; this is finally the very reason we all befriend each other, & savor our friendships like the most exquisite gifts, which they are, & mourn lost friendships somewhere inside, & at our best have, as Denny had, an endless capacity for making & keeping dear friends. We have, it turns out, infinite room in our hearts for people who make us laugh & think, people who make us reach for our best & deepest selves. We all, if we are lucky, have such boon companions. Yeats: *Think where man's glory most begins & ends, & say my glory was I had such friends.*

⌘

But it would be insulting & inaccurate too to write only hagiography of Denny; to reduce the dead to saintliness alone has always seemed reductive & dismissive. He could be a horse's ass, irritating, rude, snide, reckless, & you never met a less punctual man. On occasion his company was too strong a wine & parting was a pleasure. His questions could cut too close to the bone, his laughter could grate, his silence was sometimes oppressive, the shambles of his love life sometimes rubble heaped high, his energy sometimes a glare that hurt the eyes. & yet & yet.

⌘

He would often say to me, in his chaffing mode, that I was a stuffy & reserved soul, masked & defended, the sort of man who hid behind his dignity, both personal & professional, the sort of man who had decided, deep in the quick of his soul, that he would rather be safe & lonely than be pierced again by the shock & pain that intimacy necessarily & inevitably brings, & while I would during his lifetime protest & deflect this charge, & reply with jokes of my own, & account it, as all teasing among friends, a form of respect & affection, still it rankled then, & remains resident in my heart even now. I confess straightforwardly that I am afraid of being hurt by love, as I have been often stung in the amorous arena, &

I do not think I can bear further loss than that which I have already endured, the details of which are not germane here; & while the price of my peace is loneliness, still there is a calm in the conduct of such a life that I am loath to leave. Yet I ponder his words. He said nothing that did not have weight, even that which was uttered lightly; & there are times now when I think perhaps his lightest remarks were those with the most bone.

⤟⤞

Similarly I said to him more than once that he trod too lightly in the world, & did not have the courage to commit, & his urge to sip rather than gulp, to touch rather than hold, to wade rather than dive, was the mark of a man afraid, leery of entanglement, unwilling to live among the root of things; & while mostly those words glanced off him, there were times when they went home & he sat silently. *Is it fluidity or fear?* he said once, quietly, a remark I never forgot. But even in that case he muttered the words over his shoulder as he was walking, & I barely caught them before they whirled away like old newspapers down the street.

⤟⤞

The disposition of his remains fell to me as executor, & it seemed only right that Denny be distributed as widely & freely as possible. He was cremated in Portland, & his ashes sent (by bus) to Emanuel Hospital, Coos Bay, Sheridan, & Hibbing, Minnesota, in all of which cities small ceremonies were held for the scattering of his earthly remains. At the suggestion of the chairman of the new board of Greyhound Lines (this year a college student named Alison Moorad), a box with some of his ashes was affixed to the *Dennis Dennis*, which made a special run from New Mexico to Oregon, carrying invited guests, myself among them. Driving the bus was Hugo Sanchez, who had driven the G4500 bus on which Denny passed into the next sphere.

Alison's idea, a lovely one, was that the box be constructed & affixed to the exterior of the bus (near seat 25) in such a way that Denny sifted out little by little all the way from Albuquerque to Portland, so that somewhere along the road some of the salt he had been would circle back to where he was born mobile & restless a voyager among the endless & impatient stars. This we caused to happen, & Denny floated back into the sand & sage, & when the bus pulled into Portland, we presented the empty box to Hugo, who said that he would use it for starting his tomato plants in winter, to give them a leg up on life. This seemed like a very apt & suitable plan, especially as Hugo says he will share the tomatoes around when summer comes, a delicious & savory prospect altogether.

LUCY

He didn't see the cat until the last possible second and by then it was too late even for the usual swerve and screech of brakes, and he killed it.

No question about its death; he felt the left front tire catch the creature full-on, and then the back tire hit it too.

It seemed to have sped up right at the last second, as if it *wanted* to be hit, he thought distractedly.

He pulled over and got out heavily.

It was Lucy, the neighbor girls' cat, the cat with the half of a tail where a coyote had made a run at it and gotten an appetizer.

What with his back the way it was he couldn't even bend down or kneel down or squat to examine the body. Nor could he lift it off to the side of the road. A stick maybe, to push it off the pavement? But he couldn't bend to pick one up, nor was there anything of that sort in the car.

So he stood there staring.

It sure was dead. There was a good deal of blood—was there blood on the tire?

He was saddened and startled and regretful. It had been a sweet cat—young and foolish and exuberant, much taken with chasing up trees after the frantic cursing squirrels, and chasing after the children on their bicycles, and bringing home the heads of birds it had killed, and etc. All in all an entertaining and supple being he had rather liked finding on his picnic table, staring balefully at the splenetic squirrels.

Now there was nothing to be done but go tell his wife or the neighbors.

Already flies and a wasp had found the body and a crow floated over and soon enough the crows would be yanking out entrails.

He got back in the car and thought for a moment.

Tell the neighbor girls himself?

He quailed.

Tell his daughter, and then she could tell them?

Cowardly. Unfair pressure on the child.

Tell his wife, and then she could tell them?

I'll ask her what's right, he thought. She'll know the way to play it. She knows the neighbors better than I do.

So he drove around the corner to their house and parked and got out of the car, checking the tire for blood. He couldn't see any in the gathering darkness, which for some reason made him feel better.

Cain and Abel, he thought.

But inside the house, after he worked his way slowly up the steps, he found chaos and hubbub. The dishes were still in the sink, his son was screaming, his daughter was in tears, and his wife, furious, was mopping milk off the floor. He was sucked right into cleaning and calming and punishments for fighting and the brushing of teeth and reading of stories and a glass of wine and a light late dinner with his lovely wife, and the cat slipped out of his mind altogether, as if it had never been hit, as if it had never existed at all.

The neighbor girl found the cat herself, next morning, and there was a huge ruckus, as he heard when he got home the next night. The poor girl was heartbroken. All the children in the houses at their end of the street came over for the funeral. The cat was buried in a shoebox and the children made a headstone out of cardboard. All the children except little Nathan from next door cried, and he would have cried if he could have figured out what was going on, said his wife, who was also at the funeral.

That night after dinner as the children of the street rode their bikes up and down, some of the parents stood at the west end of the street, talking.

There was a lot of loose talk about the driver of the car who killed Lucy.

Must have been someone not from the neighborhood, said the mother of the girl. Someone from the neighborhood would have had the courage to come tell us.

Hit and run, said a father. Happens all the time.

Cat ran wild anyway, said another father cautiously.

Would have bet a dollar that she'd be hit eventually, said a mother.

We should try to get a speed bump again, said the girl's mother, which sent the conversation off onto city politics, and the icy woman who ran the Public Works, and the forms you had to fill out in fourplicate, and etc., and the death of the cat drifted away soundlessly. After a while it was too dark to see much and they called the kids in for bed.

Next day at work he had meetings all day long, one of those wasted days where you just go from meeting to meeting, and the only way to feel productive is to make notes to yourself about things to do, and while making notes to himself about things to do he wrote CAT.

He went to Mass at lunch but it didn't help.

He didn't feel bad about killing the cat, he thought, sitting in church. He felt bad that he hadn't told the neighbor girl. Now it felt too late to tell her. He could see himself at their door, confessing that he killed the cat, and their faces staring at him.

He made dinner for everyone that night and then helped his daughter with her homework and helped get his boy to bed and folded the laundry. He and his wife sat on the couch for a while pretending to read the papers but actually telling stories and laughing. This was often the best part of his day, sitting on the couch talking to her; she was so entertaining and honest, so artlessly herself, that he always felt cleansed and refreshed by her company. Even after fifteen years he still felt, nearly daily, the electric charge of affection and zest in their love affair; as if he'd met her yesterday, and was smitten all over again today. It was a strange thing, he supposed, and he had wondered many times if other men felt this way, but he no longer cared about marital patterns as a whole, no longer was curious about the nature of love in the large sense, only the nature of love on this couch, in this house, in his heart.

But even so he couldn't tell her about the cat.

Next morning he was up first, and on his way down their path to get the paper he found a dead bird, right under the mailbox.

Sparrow, looked like—what there was of it. Short beak, stubby brown body, some fluffy grayish down-feathers. Female, and a young one, too—probably just out of the nest, poor thing.

The bird's head was missing. He thought of Lucy, who left bird heads not only on her own family's porch but on his, as some sort of respectful gesture.

As he reached in the box for the paper he saw Nathan, the little neighbor boy. Nathan was maybe eighteen months old, he supposed, still a little wobbly on his fat legs, but here he was, three houses down from his home at dawn, with no mother or father in sight.

"Nathan, my man, what are you doing out here?" he asked.

As if in answer, the child sat down companionably by the mailbox.

And suddenly with no warning the man was moved to kneel—an arduous process for him, which entailed holding onto the mailbox and very slowly lowering himself down one leg at a time, until he knelt, slouched, his back burning, by the headless bird.

Nathan watched without comment.

The man opened the bird's breast, torn open by its killer, and reached in with his forefinger for some blood, and marked his own forehead with it. His glasses slid down his nose a bit and he pushed them back up and got a little blood on the bridge of his glasses, too.

Nathan reached for the bird and got some blood from its chest and put it cheerfully on the end of his nose.

"Forgive me," said the man to the boy and not to the boy, "for a death, and for my silence."

Nathan stared without comment.

A car, whizzing down the hill behind them, slowed noticeably, then whizzed away.

The man slowly hauled himself back to his feet, using the mailbox, and extended a hand to Nathan, who hauled himself up creakily in imitation, grinning.

Tucking the paper under his arm, the man walked Nathan home. Nathan's mother was horrified to find them at the door. How did he get out, he must have pushed open the screen door, I didn't know he could do that, I didn't think he was strong enough yet, thank you so much, Nathan you get in this house this minute, etc.

She didn't appear to notice the dot of blood on Nathan's nose and the man didn't say anything about it.

The man walked up the path, his back burning, and by the time he got home his son was up, so they ate breakfast together, and then he set the boy to watch Sesame Street until his wife and daughter woke, and the man got in his car to go to work, and not until he reached up to adjust the rear-view mirror did he notice that he still had blood on his brow and glasses. He wiped the blood off his brow and glasses with a piece of paper and carefully folded the paper and put it in his wallet.

I still have that piece of paper. It's between my library card and driver's license. Sometimes it falls out when I pull out a card. I used to say a prayer when it fell out but now I think the paper falling through the air is itself a prayer and so I say nothing; I just kneel slowly, using whatever I can as a prop, and pick it up, and then haul myself back up again.

PINCHING BERNIE

You want a story? I'll tell you a story. Check this out: Bernard Francis Cardinal Law, archbishop of Boston for almost twenty years, during which probably a thousand kids were raped by priests and Law knew about it but kept shuffling the rapists around from job to job and denying everything and writing letters that were total bullshit about how he knew the guys real well and saw into their hearts and their hearts were as pure as driven snow, this was while they were raping kids in sacristies and chapels and hospital rooms and classrooms and basements and cellars and billiard rooms and rectories and cabins on lakes and cars and the houses of prominent donors and beach cottages and the backs of school buses and once even in a convent, well, finally Bernie gets ridden out of town on a rail, you know, the people in the archdiocese weren't going to take this evil crap anymore, and Bernie has to vamoose from his palatial residence so fast that the coffee was still warm when the cops got there, Bernie gets rushed to the airport by true believers and put on a plane to Vatican City from where he cannot be extradited because it's its own fecking nation, that part of Rome where His Holiness the late Pope John Paul who was otherwise mostly a decent guy coddled and protected Bernie the Patron Saint of Rapists, well, Bernie, in the ancient way of churches and colleges and corporations, gets *promoted*, can you believe it, and now he's the boss of a beautiful old church in Rome, and key member of more committees and councils than you can count, and a venerated elder statesman in the Church Eternal, although he never sets foot outside the Citta del Vaticano, because he knows full well that if he sticks a toe outside the magic circle someone will grab it and haul his sorry ass out of heaven and stuff him in a jail cell in Boston so fast he wouldn't be able to spell the word criminal, which is what he is.

But that's all background. The story I want to tell you is what happened to Bernie after he vanished from the front steps of the Basilica di Santa Maria Maggiore, which you remember was a huge deal in the papers last year, **THE ABSCONDED ARCHBISHOP!, PRELATE PINCHED?, DID CARDINAL'S SINS COME HOME TO ROOST?,** that sort of headline, but no one ever found Bernie, so the Italian and American police and investigators finally officially concluded that he is probably deceased, perhaps by the hand or hands of people personally affected by the rape crisis when Bernie was the Catholic king of Boston, but more probably by criminals of one kind or another in that ancient jungle called Italy, but I am here to tell you that Bernie is alive, and I know where he is, and I know what he does all day every day, and after many months of wrangling with his minders I finally have permission to tell you and only you about what happened, because they are finally convinced that telling certain selected influential people about what happened to Bernie will somehow be a good thing, which I think is true, so here we go, although some names have been changed for obvious reasons, and I am going to have to ask you to keep this to yourself after I tell you the story, for reasons you will certainly agree are totally excellent reasons, you know what I'm saying?

❧

Let me back up a little here. Bernie started out as a regular guy. He was actually born in Mexico, son of an Air Force guy stationed in Torreon, which is smack in the middle of the country, like two hundred miles west of Monterrey, you know Monterrey, where everyone eats baby goat, that's the favorite dish, and there's music all over the place every hour of the day and night? Totally great city, I love Monterrey, not one but two great soccer teams there, the Rays and the Tigers, baby. Great city.

Anyway, Bernie's smart as a whip as a kid, and eventually he goes to Harvard, and then joins the priests, and gets sent to Mississippi, where he edits the Catholic newspaper and is actually a pretty good dude, big on civil rights, a real accomplished young priest, although even then there were people who thought Bernie had a slightly larger ego than was technically called for, but hey, he was still just a kid, and kids have to show off before they get a grip and realize what real accomplishment is, which has nothing to do with flash and dash, you know what I'm saying?

At age forty-two Bernie gets named a bishop and gets sent to Missouri, where he continues to be a fairly decent guy by most accounts, looking out for Vietnamese priests fleeing the Commies, and trying to work out peace treaties with the Jews and the Presbies and Episcopals, he even works out a deal where Episcopal priests who were married with kids could work in Catholic dioceses, which was how something you hardly ever see happened here and there, a priest making out with his wife on the beach, and barking at his kids that he would *stop this car and turn around if there was any more fighting in the back seat!* and weeping copious at the wedding of his daughter to some dope with a mohawk and a Mustang, and stuff like that.

Anyway Bernie finally gets named Archbishop of Boston, this is in 1984, and a year later our man John Paul makes Bernie a cardinal, which is as high as you can go without shoving John Paul off the pope's chair, which there were not a few people who thought this was Bernie's not-so-secret ambition, to be master of the universe, His Holiness Bernie the First, but first of all John Paul didn't die mysteriously like his predecessor the first John Paul did—you can't kill a Pole as easy as you can an Italian—and second of all Bernie crashed and burned in Boston, and had to high-tail it to the airport, and etc. as above.

So that's the basic outline. You can read all sorts of stuff about what Bernie did when he was bishop and archbishop and cardinal, this statement and that, this policy and that, this news conference and that, and Bernie never missed a chance to preen for the camera, he wasn't shy, our boy Bernie, even in freefall, he thought he could bluff his way out of it, and he was very hip to the fact that the more people who knew about him the higher his profile would be in the old College of Cardinals when it was time to fill John Paul's chair, as eventually it would be, not even Poles live forever, as Bernie well knew. But he did a lot of other things too, some of them cool and excellent things that didn't get much public play, and you can be cynical about that, and say that he hadn't learned the oily craft yet, and that's why there are no puff pieces in the archives, but the fact is that he was a decent guy in a lot of ways. I mean, hell, he became a priest, which isn't exactly the easiest road to money and power, and very often is a decision to be a servant for life. What I am trying to say is that he wasn't always a slime bag, and that for a long time, in a lot of ways, Bernie was a regular guy, maybe even tending toward excellent.

೦৵৹

But he became the slime bag's slime bag, an all-pro slime bag. Let's review some of his greatest hits. Father Paul Shanley, pastor of Saint Jean's and Saint John the Evangelist, raped more kids than anyone can count, from ages six to eighteen. Every time somebody complained, Bernie moved him to another parish. Finally he traded him to a parish in California, like in a baseball deal. You wonder if he got a player to be named later. Or Father John Geoghan, another winner. Priest at, successively, Blessed Sacrament, Saint Bernard's, Saint Paul's, Saint Andrew's, Saint Brendan's, and Saint Julia's. Nailed more than a hundred children, some of them as young as three years old. Every time there was a complaint or a rumor, Bernie moved him to a new parish. Imagine how much fun it must have been to have a parish tea for the new priest, and shake his hand, and say how lovely to have you in our faith community, Father!, and then discover he's diddling your toddler at the parish picnic. Lovely. And Bernie just kept slapping new labels on the guy and mailing him to a new parish. Father Bob Gale, who raped kids *on the altar*. Father Dan Graham, who raped kids, people complained directly to Bernie, and Bernie *promotes him to be in charge of nineteen parishes*, whoa. Or good old Father Joe Birmingham—Our Lady of Fatima, Saint James, Saint Michael's, Saint Columbkille's, Saint Ann's, Saint Brigid's, get the picture how many parishes he was in, wonder why? and, in a lovely touch from Bernie, chaplain of the juvenile court in Brighton, on the west side of the city, on the recommendation of the Cardinal Archbishop of Boston, Bernard Francis Cardinal Law. So incredibly apt, eh, that you would recommend a guy who raped at least fifty children to be the chaplain for the court where troubled kids go? But that was Bernie for you. No flies on Bernie. Somebody complains that good old Father Joe was caught raping a child ten months old, a child who hadn't even learned to walk yet, and Bernie gently moves him along to a new parish, and never says a word to anyone. How lovely to have you in our faith community, Father! Would you like our children served up on a platter, so you can commit unimaginable perversions upon them, and twist their brains and guts and souls into knots that never heal, and plant the seeds of horror in families that will squirm for a hundred years, or would you like to pluck them one by one on your own good time? Will His Eminence the Cardinal also be joining us for tea?

❧

Anyway Bernie finally heard the hounds of hell barking and he goes pell-mell for the airport, boarding a direct flight to Rome from Boston, and gets set up at the Basilica di Santa Maria Maggiore, which is a hell of a huge beautiful church in Rome, the pope uses it sometimes for Masses and shows, it's a pile of a thing, nearly two thousand years old, and there Bernie holds court like the old days, he gets chauffeured around in a big black car, and he has servants and cooks and a valet, and he sits on this council and that, making quiet pronouncements on education and the holiness of the family, you wonder why his lips don't fall off when he says the words *holiness of the family*, or how come God the Father doesn't make it automatic that whenever Bernie says something fatuous about the family, all the kids who got raped on his watch immediately shout inside his head, wouldn't that be cool? If *I* was lord of the universe that's what I'd do.

But whatever. Anyway the point is that Bernie is now resident in what is basically a castle, which has a lot of remote rooms and obscure corners, and while there are a few security guys, they are not real intense about it, because everyone thinks Bernie has diplomatic immunity, no one can touch him inside the Vatican City, and he's real careful not to come out, it's not like he's going to accept an honorary doctorate or give a speech ever again in these United States, so things look pretty good for Bernie, looks like the fire's dying down, the poor bastard who succeeded Bernie in Boston, a Franciscan named Sean Patrick O'Malley, good Irish boy from Ohio, he's cooling things down, he's a straight shooter, O'Malley is, and despite the fact that the archdiocese now is penniless and shutting down grade schools because of shelling out untold millions of dollars to the families of the kids who got diddled three times a day by Bernie's boys, looks like everything will just be what it is until Bernie kicks the bucket and there's a momentous funeral and his body is laid in some crypt in Rome and there's a rash of stories in the papers and the memories finally piss away and the whole thing becomes two lines in official histories, you know, like 2002: Bernard Cardinal Law resigns as Archbishop of Boston because of sexual abuse allegations. Sexual Abuse Allegations, Jesus, could you get more weak-ass words than those?

~⊙~

But then one Sunday morning at Gate of Heaven parish in South Boston the priest is going on about forgiveness, and he says Only the Lord has the right to forgive those accused of crimes against children, and my friend Jimmy snaps. He stands up and says quietly, that's crap, and he walks out of the church. He goes home and says to his wife Rosemary that he has to see a guy about a guy, he'll be back in a couple of weeks, a business trip, and she knows him well enough to know that this is something really important, something he has to do, she can tell from his face, and she trusts him enough that she doesn't say anything except I love you Jimmy, and call me when you can, and try to be back by the beginning of school because the twins are starting fifth grade and I don't think I can help them with their math homework this year, but you can, right? This makes him smile, angry as he is, and after he packs his stuff and gets the car out of the garage he goes back in and leaves a note under the toaster that she is the coolest woman there ever was and he still can't believe she married him, is he dreaming or what? Then he drives up to Charlestown and talks to a guy and a few hours later he and the guy are on a plane to Rome, and basically from this point on Bernie's goose is cooked.

∼⦿∾

One time I asked Jimmy what happened when he snapped that day at Gate of Heaven, and he says, Let me put it this way. I got a daughter and two sons. Somebody sticks their pecker in my daughter, and he's not wearing the wedding ring she gave him at the altar under the beaming gaze of the father of the bride, we got us a problem, and if that someone is a priest, and she trusted him to not touch the temple of her body, and he's playing mind games about power and religion and God's will and evil crap like that, we got us a problem the size of a bullet, you know what I'm saying? Same with my boys. Someone sticks a pecker in one or both of my sons, and that pecker don't belong to someone who has joyously been united to my boy in the civil ceremony recently approved by the legislature of the state of Massachusetts, a civil ceremony conducted under the confused gaze of the father of the groom, we got us a problem, and even then I got a problem, but that's my personal problem, which my wife says I have to get over if I am to be consistent about love being the biggest frog in the pond regardless of gender.

But what really got me that day, says Jimmy, was the priest at Mass says Only the Lord has the right to forgive a guy who raped an infant, and right there I think, o no no no. That's crap. Only the mother has the right to even try to forgive such a slime crime as that. Maybe the father, but any decent father is spending the rest of his life thinking what size pieces to cut the slime bag into, stew meat for the lions at the zoo or fillets for the sharks in the aquarium? The Lord has nothing to do with this. The Lord don't play. The mother plays. And I know a mother whose kid got raped by a guy Bernie covered up for. She lives two blocks over. The kid's a wreck, the father's a wreck, the mother's trying to hold the family together, and Bernie gets promoted and goes to live in a castle? No no no. No way. So I figure it's time to correct the situation, you know what I'm saying?

※

It's easier to pinch an archbishop than maybe you think. Consider the situation. He gets driven around in a big black car, he wanders around alone in a huge house, he is no spring chicken who is going to sprint away from people who want to borrow his company for a while, and he's not the kind of guy who packs major weaponry. So when Jimmy and his friend get to the Basilica di Santa Maria Maggiore and scout it out, they take a few days and do it right, find a guy who knows a guy who shows them building plans and such, and they have a chat with the family of the driver, and get the deal on each of the servants, and get a grip on Bernie's schedule, and map out routes he takes to each of the committees and councils he sits on, well, they have enough information to make things happen, and one evening as His Eminence Bernard Francis Cardinal Law sets out to go to dinner in the Prati neighborhood, his driver pauses a moment in a dimly lit street and His Eminence is escorted into another vehicle and the driver is gently chloroformed after he parks the car. A passerby discovers the driver, calls the police, hoopla ensues, cardinal kidnapped, the Mafia suspected, Italy in an uproar, pope issues statement, there are many meetings and press conferences and such, but Bernie never actually does get found, and after a while the papers move along to the next scandal, and His Holiness Pope Benedict the Sixteenth, a canny old politico, handles the problem by offering a big public Mass for the safety of Bernard his brother in Christ, and then he quietly appoints an interim archpriest of the Basilica di Santa Maria Maggiore, and everybody moves along.

∽∾

The problem with nicking a guy from one country and bringing him into another isn't the take, which as you see above was cupcake stuff, but the international borders, which is a serious problem ever since Old Towelhead murdered three thousand people in New York and then nearly peed himself cackling in glee, talk about your seventh circle of hell, he'll be down there playing cards with Mao and Hitler and Stalin and Father John Geoghan soon enough, the chortling bastard. Anyway how they moved Bernie was interesting—they got him to the coast, where they had arranged for shipping, and then Jimmy and his friend and Bernie all piled into a big container which was supposed to be filled with wine, but which Jimmy had arranged to be like a little lake cabin, with bunks, water, food, books, and other necessities for three men traveling by ship across the Atlantic Ocean. When the ship unloaded, this was in Charlestown, some containers were examined by Homeland Security and customs, but theirs was not, for several thousand reasons, and so Bernard Francis Cardinal Law returned to the Archdiocese of Boston, unbeknownst to Sean Patrick Cardinal O'Malley or anyone else except Jimmy and the guy from Charlestown.

When Jimmy told me this story I was fascinated by the books, and I asked him what books they had, and he smiled and said his friend from Charlestown was a *huge* Dennis Lehane fan and he had four Lehane novels, whereas Jimmy took advantage of the free time and read the South American magic realists he had heard a lot about but never read, Jorge Amado and Gabriel Garcia Marquez, though he said he also brought a Mario Vargas Llosa but just could not get into it, it was totally boring, last time you catch me reading a novel from Peru, man. The Cardinal, said Jimmy, pissed and moaned the first few days but finally read the Lehanes. Jimmy says no one said much to each other, for all sorts of reasons, and there were no dramatic incidents or conversations or anything. Just sleeping and reading, pretty much, says Jimmy. We took turns sleeping so we could keep a sharp eye on Bernie. It was actually kind of a vacation, you know what I'm saying?

 ~&~

Once back in Boston they took Bernie to see a surgeon who did some cosmetic work and donated it to the cause, and Bernie got fitted for some uniforms also donated by a guy, and then Bernie went to work, and that's basically the end of the story, because what happened to His Eminence Bernard Francis Cardinal Law is that he works seven days a week, twelve hours a day, no weekends off, no vacations, and that's what he'll do until the day he has a heart attack and wins a date in hell with Mao and the boys.

The details of Bernie's work schedule are not something I can share with you for reasons you can understand, but suffice it to say that Bernie's job is cleaning the bathrooms of the mothers whose kids got raped when Bernie was the boss. There were probably a thousand kids raped in the Archdiocese over the years, before and during Bernie's time, and that's a lot of bathrooms for a guy seventy-seven years old to be scrubbing on his hands and knees, but if he gets through the first thousand toilets and bathtubs, says Jimmy, then back he goes to the first one again and starts over. There's a real sophisticated arrangement whereby Bernie is supervised and shuttled from house to house and fed and looked after by a couple doctors so he doesn't punk out, and Jimmy gives him a little pep talk sometimes when he looks like his productivity is flagging, and that's pretty much the story. Jimmy says the best part about the whole thing is the day he came home to Rosemary and he found a note she wrote him under the toaster, what a woman, he says, my God, can you believe she married me?

Here and there someone who you tell this story to in confidence will say Jeeeeesus, isn't that hard on the old man, twelve hours a day on his knees up to the armpits in shit, not to mention kidnapping, and to people like that I say what Jimmy says, which is any time you feel the slightest hint of feeling for Bernie, imagine a kid, just one kid of the thousand kids you could choose, a kid absolutely terrified, let's say he's six years old, he's in *kindergarten* for Chrissake, he just learned to painstakingly write his whole name in block letters, and he's trapped in a dank room somewhere, and there's a big priest with pockmarks on his face pulling his pants down and waving his dick and smiling ravenously at the kid, you imagine *that*. So any time you feel the slightest bad for Bernie, you think about that kindergarten kid, and suddenly old Bernie crawling around on his knees the rest of his life up to the armpits in shit don't seem like a bad idea, it seems like the absolute *best* idea, you know what I'm saying?

BIN LADEN'S BLIND SPOT

Once before I told you a story about being the barber in the cave of Osama bin Laden, son of Alia Ghanem and Muhammad bin Laden, and about the bald spot the size of a baby's fist on the back of his head, shaped *exactly* like Iceland, complete with the Vestfjarda Peninsula to the west, which he does *not* like to speak of, and about how my noting this bald spot led to the ban on me speaking aloud while on duty in the cave, which is not a duty I volunteered for, exactly, but that is another story. The story I want to tell you now is about something that happened in the cave one day.

There are fifteen men who live in the cave complex on a regular basis, and another twenty or so who have regular business with Himself, and while they are all devout Muslims, you cannot live in a cave with a large number of men for years and years without developing affections and detestations, and finally two of the men fell in love with each other, and after a great deal of thinking and discussing, they asked Osama to marry them. You can imagine the roar with which he greeted this request, and in fact he lost his temper so thoroughly that he had to cancel a video production he had been writing and rewriting for weeks, for which the props had just arrived, the right sort of rifle and wrinkled fatigue jacket and that sort of thing.

Osama wanted to issue an execution edict on the spot but his subcommanders pointed out that technically no crime had as yet been committed that anyone knew of, so far this was affection rather than abomination, and also one of the men was Osama's driver, the only man in the cave who knew how to drive a stick shift, and without the driver no one could drive the truck that delivered actors and props to the site where they filmed the videos, and then where would they be? No videos, no glorious revolution, am I right?

I sat silent while they argued about this all night long. One thing no one ever admits about Muslims is that they are chatterboxes of the first order, willing and able to talk all night long and argue about the tiniest nuttiest things, like the time Osama went into a hissy fit that lasted for days because he lost an argument about whether chess was the work of the devil, which of course it isn't, although it was invented by the Hindus or Buddhists, who are all going to hell apparently because they are not Muslims. I am myself not Muslim, but I am a very good barber, and while I am sure they are sure I am going to hell, I am sure I am not going to hell, because I have never done any of the things they have done, and from what I have seen of what they have done they are most definitely going to hell. For example I once saw Osama poring over a list of the poor people who were roasted to death in America on September 11, and on that list there were many children, and he never said one prayer for any of them, or apologized for their murders, or did anything but smile as he made little check marks by their names, counting up victims of the glorious revolution. Now there is a man going to hell on the express train.

Anyway his driver and the other man started holding hands when they walked around the cave, which drove the Sheik insane, but they never kissed or did anything else that would provoke fatwah, and indeed their respect and affection for each other soon began to have a salutary effect, and elevate morale, and humanize life in the cave, which before had been pretty much military and religious edict all day and night. I suppose that their friendly banter, and the way they really liked each other's company, reminded everyone what life could be, and maybe had been for some men—some of them were so young and impressionable that I am sure they had never known any other life but that of soldier in the glorious revolution, which had led them to scuttling through a cave complex in what must be the hottest driest mountains on this holy earth.

Well, if I was a storyteller, which I am not, I would conclude this story with some important event, or a lesson of some sort, but this is actually the end of the story, and the story is about how two men holding hands changed the very air in the cave where the Sheik is hiding. Ever since the driver and the other man fell in love with each other there has been much more laughter and friendliness in the cave, and I am beginning to think that whatever it is the Sheik wants so desperately to happen outside the cave, the reason he murdered those little children, is not going to happen, because the more the men laugh and are friendly, the angrier the Sheik gets, but there are more men than there are sheiks, so I think in the end the numbers are against Himself. He gives long speeches that go on for hours and hours about the sin and abomination of two men falling in love with each other, but I think this has nothing to do with what he calls unnatural passions, and everything to do with the fact that all the men in the cave would rather, in the end, laugh than murder children. I have to say that I think the Sheik is going to lose his war in the end because there is not enough laughing in the world he wants to make, and who wants to live in that world? It's bad enough that we have to live in this cave with him.

BIOGRAPHICAL NOTE

Brian Doyle is the editor of *Portland Magazine* at the University of Portland, in Oregon, and the author of ten books of essays, nonfiction, "proems," and the sprawling novel *Mink River.* His work has appeared in the annual *Best American Essays, Best Science & Nature Writing,* and *Best Spiritual Writing* anthologies. He received the American Academy of Arts and Letters Award in Literature in 2008, for murky reasons.